## A PROPER DISTANCE

A hint of a smile tugged at one corner of her mouth. She suppressed it by pursing her lips. Her look simulated censure, but she gave him a short nod of assent.

As he led her inside, he glanced back to his mother and got one last glimpse of the duchess crossing her arms over her chest. “Please excuse us, ma’am.”

When they reached the dance floor, Miss Irvine let out a giggle. “I fear your mother is going to have much to say to you about this, your grace.”

“On the contrary, I’m hoping it will teach her to know when to keep her opinions to herself.”

Adrian took her in his arms, careful to maintain a proper distance between them. Still, her proximity intoxicated him. Her waist felt impossibly slender, and the soft curve of her back beneath his hand drove him to distraction.

A trace of rosewater grazed his nose, and the light of a thousand candles whirled by to add to the headiness of the experience. His mind reeled with mixed emotions.

*She would have kissed me,* he thought, looking into her eyes.

# THE ARTFUL MISS IRVINE

*Jennifer Malin*

ZEBRA BOOKS
Kensington Publishing Corp.
http://www.kensingtonbooks.com

ZEBRA BOOKS are published by

Kensington Publishing Corp.
850 Third Avenue
New York, NY 10022



All Kensington titles, imprints and distributed lines are available at special quantity discounts for bulk purchases for sales promotion, premiums, fund-raising, educational or institutional use.

Special book excerpts or customized printings can also be created to fit specific needs. For details, write or phone the office of the Kensington Special Sales Manager: Kensington Publishing Corp., 850 Third Avenue, New York, NY 10022. Attn. Special Sales Department. Phone: 1-800-221-2647.



First Printing: September 2003
10 9 8 7 6 5 4 3 2 1

Printed in the United States of America

# One

Maeve Irvine stood on the deck of the ship, her heart beating fast while the crewmen completed the mooring. Impatient to start exploring England, she took in what little she could see from the ship—a view of the London wharf. Wisps of late-morning fog swirled around the brick warehouses and cobblestone street, lending a mystical quality to an otherwise drab scene. The dinginess of the buildings didn't lessen her excitement. She was used to docks, having accompanied her late father many times in Boston while he oversaw his shipping interests.

She turned to her companion, Miss Grey, a woman who had once been her nurse and currently served as an abigail. "So far London doesn't look much different from home, does it, Grey?"

The older woman squinted at their surroundings and wrinkled her longish nose. "Home was never this smelly."

Maeve laughed. "Obviously, you didn't spend much time at the docks."

"No, I can't say I did." Miss Grey met her gaze and broke into a smile. "One thing I will say, Miss—'tis good to see you looking happy again."

"Who wouldn't be happy at the prospect of setting foot on land after a month at sea?" Glancing back at the dock, she saw the crew extending planks to the pier below. She drew in a breath and added, "Not to mention the prospect of a whole new life."

"Certainly the worst is behind us." The abigail set a hand on her shoulder. "You should be proud of how you've conducted yourself over the past year, Miss. With no help except for the solicitor's, you settled your father's estate and liquidated all of his assets. You even escaped the hands of all the fortune hunters who hounded you after Mr. Irvine's death."

"One of those escapes was rather narrow, though." A lump formed in Maeve's throat, and her smile faltered—but only for an instant. "Still, none of that matters now. No fortune hunters will haunt me here. My aunt has agreed to keep quiet about my financial situation. With any luck, everyone will assume I'm coming to live with her out of necessity. I've even let on to a few people aboard ship that I hope to make a living painting portraits."

Miss Grey frowned. "Are you sure you don't want it known that you at least have a dowry? Otherwise, you may have no suitors at all. You can let it slip that you're not destitute without disclosing the full extent of your fortune."

She shook her head. "I'm not looking for suitors. At three-and-twenty, I've accepted that I'm on the shelf. My fulfillment in life will have to come from my artwork. Aunt Blaine has promised to introduce me to some of my late uncle's painter colleagues. I hope to learn much from them."

"But, Miss, you're not on the shelf at all—"

"Ah, I see they're allowing passengers to disembark," Maeve interrupted. The fact of her spinsterhood hadn't been easy to swallow, but she had managed. Now she had nothing more to say on the subject. "Let's go."

Miss Grey hesitated. "As you wish, Miss."

Maeve glided down the planks, the abigail mincing behind her. As she set foot on British soil for the first time, she looked back to see if the crew had begun unloading cargo. Instead she spotted a friend she'd made during the voyage. Viscount Faraday emerged above deck, adjusting the shoulder pads on his well-tailored but dull gray jacket.

She waved both arms and called, "Lord Faraday! Down here."

He pinpointed her and nodded, then started down the ramp with as unsure a foot as Miss Grey.

Maeve stifled a giggle. She didn't mean to laugh at this man, who had been kind to her during their voyage, but today her spirits were fairly brimming over.

His lordship progressed at a snail's pace, a sliver of sunlight cutting through the fog and reflecting off his sparsely haired head. At last, he joined them on terra firma. "Good morning, Miss Irvine, Miss Grey. How fortunate to see you one last time before we part. I was sorry to miss the pleasure of breaking fast with you this morning."

"We missed you, too," Maeve said. "Were you unwell again?"

"I'm afraid so—and doubly distressed to lose my final chance to dine with you." His narrow shoulders sagged. "I shall miss the cozy shipboard meals we've shared."

Another giggle bubbled up inside of her. "A gallant comment, to be sure, my lord. On many evenings those 'cozy' meals slid all about the table—or got tossed around in our stomachs after we'd eaten. Besides, you can still dine with us here in London, and the setting will be far more pleasant."

He shook his head. "I fear you'll have little time for

me once you settle in and all the young bucks begin to court you."

"Oh, la." Maeve waved off his comment. Why did everyone insist she would have suitors? "You know I'm here to seek a career in art, not a husband."

"We shall see how you feel in a few weeks."

Under other circumstances his persistence might have vexed her, but now she was too excited to pay him heed. She gave him a wry look. "I daresay I'm not as susceptible to the opposite sex as you seem to believe."

At that moment a peal of hearty laughter rang out in the street a few yards away. She turned to see a pair of handsome young men passing by. The first wore the smart regimentals of the English army, his red coat set off by his straw-colored hair. His companion, however, was the one who made her breath catch. Dressed in a crisp navy blue jacket filled well by his broad shoulders, he had a shock of dark brown hair and a strong but straight nose. His slate gray breeches delineated the ample muscles of his thighs, and his black Hessian boots gleamed from a recent polishing.

Still grinning at whatever joke he and his friend had shared, he fixed his twinkling dark eyes on her.

As he held her gaze, her lips curved instinctively.

He widened his smile and nodded to her.

The familiar treatment made her realize how inappropriate her expression must be. *Goodness, he must think me forward!* She snapped her attention back to Lord Faraday.

The viscount gave her a soft smile. "You belong with a fine young fellow."

Embarrassed by her lapse, she looked down at her feet. "As I've told you, I plan to live my life independently . . . supporting myself through portrait painting."

"Well, I wish you the best in that and more, my dear."

He looked over his shoulder at the ship. "Forgive me, but I shall have to leave you ladies for a short time to oversee the transfer of my luggage from ship to coach. While I'm at it, I'll locate your trunks, too, and secure a respectable hackney to carry you to your aunt's."

"You needn't go to so much trouble for us, my lord," Maeve said. "I handled such matters on the other side of the ocean. There's no reason I can't do the same here."

"No trouble at all, Miss Irvine." He bowed. "Should you need anything in my absence, please apply to Captain Singer."

She smiled. "Thank you for your kindness—all of it."

"My pleasure." He excused himself and hurried away.

Maeve turned to watch the activity on the ship, trying to see if she could spot her trunks being unloaded. Some of the crew rolled barrels out of the hull, while others took down sails and reeled fat ropes into coils. A third group of men tackled the boards of the deck with mops, scrub brushes, and buckets of soapy water.

"Looks as though we can expect a good long wait," she said to Miss Grey.

After a few minutes of standing about, she and the abigail fashioned seats for themselves among some large crates on the pier. Squeezed in amidst the cargo, they could survey the scene without being readily observed themselves.

A quarter hour passed, and Maeve began to regret that she'd packed away her sketchbook, but the unwieldy item would have been awkward to carry. Then she remembered that she had another source of diversion on hand. Looking in her reticule, she pulled out a slim volume of Shakespeare.

"Perhaps *Troilus and Cressida* can help us pass the time," she said to Miss Grey, opening to a marked page.

"Do you recall the play I started reading to you the other night during the storm?"

The woman slid her a sideways glance. "Yes, Miss, but you know I'm not a great admirer of Shakespeare. I have trouble understanding the people in those plays. They all talk so strange-like."

Maeve nodded in sympathy. "Shakespeare is difficult until one grows accustomed to the language. Would you rather not hear any more?"

Her forehead furrowed. "Perhaps you could simply tell me the story in your own words. That might help me understand why *you* fancy the play so much."

"Gladly." Maeve closed the volume and leaned back against a barrel, her gaze drifting up to the clearing sky. "I must admit the plot is somewhat peculiar, but what intrigues me is all of the passion in the play. Each character has someone he or she desires so much, and when a love is finally requited, it is done with such intensity. One can feel the profound degrees of desire and, in turn, contentment. I've never before read anything of the like."

Miss Grey's eyes rounded. "Truly, Miss, from what you're telling me, I reckon your father wouldn't have *let* you read anything like it."

"Whether Papa would have approved or not is impossible to say, but surely at my age I'm mature enough to read Shakespeare." Maeve stretched out her legs, crossing them at the ankles. "Anyway, the play takes place during the Trojan War. As you know, the conflict started when a Trojan man named Paris abducted the Spartan queen, Helen, and refused to return her to King Menelaus."

Miss Grey leaned closer, propping her elbow on an adjacent barrel and putting her chin in her hand. "I was wondering why they kept mentioning Paris and Greece together. Isn't Paris in France?"

"Indeed it is. *This* Paris, however, is a man—a big, brave soldier whose love for Helen was so strong that he fought a war to keep her."

The abigail smiled. "And was she just as sweet on him?"

"Oh, yes, in the play she certainly is." Maeve tilted her head to one side. "Helen has this wonderful, lazy, satisfied air about her. Unlike some of the other characters, she shows no desperate longing—only pure, knowing contentment, even as a horrific war rages on around her. A thousand ships, thousands of lives, bloodshed . . . all of it merely so she and Paris can be together."

"A love that stirred up all of that fuss must have been something indeed."

"Yes. I daresay *she* had no trouble adjusting to life in a new country. Neither would I, if I had a handsome abductor to take care of me." Maeve let her head drop back on the barrel behind her. Facing the sky, she closed her eyes. Unbidden, a face popped into her mind—that of the unknown man in the street who had smiled at her a short while ago.

She sighed. He was such a handsome devil—likely just the sort to break a woman's heart. Good looks could hide a lot of inner ugliness, she'd learned. Luckily for her, she wasn't apt to run into this fellow again.

At that moment some sixth sense made her blink her eyes open. To her shock, the man in question was towering over her from behind the barrel that supported her head.

Yes, this was the woman he'd seen earlier—the one he knew from *somewhere*. Adrian Heywood, Duke of Ashton, looked into an upside-down pair of eyes the color of the Mediterranean Sea. It occurred to him that a well-bred lady shouldn't have been languishing around the docks in such a seductive manner. Sailors weren't known for their scruples when it came to the fair sex.

"Oh!" She jerked into an upright position and twisted around to look at him.

"I beg your pardon." He stepped around her side so she could see him more easily. Unfortunately, he still couldn't place her. He recalled her large blue eyes and the pin-straight blond hair that threatened to escape the bun on her head. His gaze slipped downward before he schooled it back up to meet hers. Surely he should have remembered her pert breasts and slim waist, but they didn't offer him any further insight. "I didn't mean to startle you."

A rosy tinge seeped into her ivory cheeks. She had the beauty of a statue but the glow of a living woman. Odd how she seemed so familiar . . . and yet somehow unfamiliar.

"That's quite all right. I was just . . . er, lost in my reading." Her accent was strange—rather flat. The pink in her cheeks deepened, and she held up a book—closed, he noted. "Sometimes when I read Shakespeare I get carried away."

He couldn't recall ever hearing such enunciation. Where on earth did he know her from? He bowed a greeting. "The docks can be dangerous for unattended women. I saw your escort leave and thought I'd better join you and your companion."

She raised her eyebrows. "How considerate."

"Not at all. Forgive me for not waiting on you before. I had to ensure that a certain urgent shipment got under way, or I would have come over as soon as I recognized you."

"Recognized me?" She looked at him more closely, her eyes narrowing.

He took her expression for one of suspicion. So she'd already gleaned that he couldn't recall her name. Now *his* cheeks heated. He forced himself to hold her gaze, but he didn't quite know how to explain his stupidity.

She cocked an eyebrow and waited for him to go on.

Unsure what to say, he gave her a self-conscious smile.

Her lips tugged at the corners, and he realized—to his surprise—that his predicament amused her. Thank heaven she wasn't insulted.

"I hope you'll still be smiling when I make this next admission," he said finally. "There is nothing for it but to confess. I cannot for the life of me remember your name. Naturally, such a face as yours has made an indelible record in my mind, but I cannot quite place where or when I've seen you before."

Her mouth twitched as if she were struggling not to grin. She moistened her lips. "A lady does not like to be so readily forgotten."

Her tone confirmed she was amused, and all tension fled his body. In this situation, most fashionable young women he knew would have cut him dead. Who was she? Studying her features, he tried desperately to jog his memory. "Give me a hint."

A throat clearing beside her turned their attention to her companion. The older woman sat stiff and wild-eyed, obviously not diverted but alarmed.

The younger woman rolled her eyes, then turned back to him, her countenance more serious. "I believe my abigail wishes to remind me of the perils of speaking to strangers. I hope you will excuse us?"

He pursed his lips. "You know very well that we're not strangers."

She laughed—a throaty chuckle that warmed his heart. "When you can prove as much by remembering who I am, you shall have to call on me more often. I shouldn't want you to forget me again. Until then, I'm afraid you must consider me a stranger."

He eyed her a moment longer. "I can't fathom why my wits are so dull today. I'm usually quite good with names. Won't you take pity and enlighten me?"

"I'm afraid I cannot." She gave him a mischievous smile.

"Miss, please—" her maid said.

The young woman held up a finger at her. "One moment, Grey. This gentleman is just taking his leave."

The abigail's uneasiness gave him pause. Perhaps she had a point and her mistress was wrong to tease him, yet he couldn't help but find the treatment amusing. He'd forgotten how exhilarating a saucy look from an attractive woman could be. The fascination he felt for the mysterious blonde startled him. He shouldn't have been playing this game any more than she.

He sighed. "Well, given my lax manners, I suppose your silence is only fair. But I swear I shall remember you—probably the moment I leave the docks."

"Then I shall expect you to call on me tomorrow." Her smile wavered a little and took on a wistful quality.

*She doesn't believe I'll be able to place her,* he thought, *and she truly wants me to visit.* Another unexpected wave of excitement swelled inside of him. In the two years since Belinda's death, no other woman had tempted him to pursue her.

"You are staying in London?" he asked.

"Miss," the maid broke in, her tone stern.

Still focusing on him, the blonde bit her lower lip. "I'm afraid I can't tell you any more."

He nodded, gazing into her eyes one last time. "Very

well. I shall do all in my power to call on you tomorrow morning."

She gave him a faint smile.

Taking up her hand, he bowed. Her fingers were slim and soft, her skin cool to the touch. Reluctantly, he let them slide from his. He nodded to her companion, who gave him a stony stare. Then he turned away.

As he left the pier, his mind reeled. His memory lapse perplexed him, but eventually he would figure out how he knew her. What astonished him was that he'd actually promised to call on her. Was he truly prepared for such a step? Belinda's betrayal had left him so bitter that he'd vowed he would never again marry. It followed that he had no occasion to bestow attentions on any woman.

He glanced back over his shoulder toward the enigmatic blonde, now some twenty yards away. Her gaze met his, and she looked away quickly.

Turning back around, he crossed the street. It wasn't that he'd never reexamined his vow against marriage. His mother took every opportunity to remind him he had no direct heir to his title, only a daughter who might not even bear his blood. For years he'd been fending off Mother's pressures to seek a new wife, to attend more social engagements, *at least* to dance at small parties given near their country seat.

Now he found himself longing to call on a woman, one whose name and address he didn't even know. Perhaps that was part of her appeal.

*Who is she?* He racked his brain. When he and his friend Denny McDowell had passed her earlier, Denny had said she didn't look familiar to him. Adrian supposed he'd have to describe her to some other acquaintances and see if anyone had an idea.

What if no one did? Lord, but he hoped he didn't

have to resort to asking his mother. He wasn't sure he was ready to go that far.

The thought depressed him. The blonde at the pier had seemed so full of life—in contrast to him. Her eyes radiated impish enjoyment. What other woman he knew would have accepted his defective memory with such good humor?

He glanced toward the pier one last time, but now a building blocked his view. For a split second, he had an urge to run back and beg for more information.

*Nonsense.* For all he knew, when he remembered who she was he wouldn't even want to see her again. Her playful manner could be the tip of a deep streak of lasciviousness. Perhaps he knew her because she'd been mistress to one of his friends.

But he didn't think so. Her prudish companion had the air of a protective governess overseeing a well-bred charge.

Clinging to that thought, he found himself hoping the blonde was respectable. Her mischievous behavior had been a pleasant surprise, and it had been a long time since *anything* had surprised him. That little difference had made him feel alive again, made him believe that life still held possibilities. How long had it been since he'd felt that way?

When he reached his carriage, he decided to make a brief stop before he went to collect his mother and daughter. He hoped someone at his club would be able to help spur his memory. When he ascertained the blonde's identity, he *would* call on her, despite his apprehensions. He had promised to visit her tomorrow, and he would keep his word . . . and think no further about his motives.

# Two

Maeve climbed the front steps of the grand brownstone town house where her aunt lived. At the top, she stopped and waited for Miss Grey to catch up. For the first time since she'd decided to move to London, she felt apprehensive. Six months ago, with no family left in Boston, she'd figured she had nothing to lose. Now she wondered what her life here would be like, living with an aunt she'd never met.

" 'Tis a palace," Miss Grey whispered from behind her.

She followed the maid's gaze up to the façade of the house. The baroque ornamentation made Boston's finest architecture appear utilitarian in comparison. "Well suited to a countess, I suppose."

Her stomach fluttering, she lifted the knocker and rapped at the door. Though Lady Blaine had written multiple assurances of her welcome, Maeve couldn't help but wonder if the rapport they'd built through correspondence would stand up in person. Would the woman prove stuffy? Could the quaint manners of an American possibly live up to the expectations of the British nobility? She hoped her aunt was as forgiving an aristocrat as her shipboard friend, Viscount Faraday.

A liveried butler answered and looked down his thin

nose at her card. He gave her a nod. "Come in, Miss Irvine. I'll inform her ladyship of your arrival."

He ushered her and Miss Grey into a cavernous foyer and vanished through a pair of doors up the hall and to the left.

While they waited, Maeve surveyed the wide passageway ahead of them. Niches filled with statuary lined the wood-paneled walls, leading to a vast curving staircase at the back of the house. Intricate carvings adorned the woodwork, and everything gleamed as though freshly polished.

"My compliments to the housekeeper," she murmured.

"Oh, my, she is here already?" a woman's voice carried through the open doors the butler had entered. "Send her in, of course, Webster."

The man reappeared and flung the doors open wider. "Lady Blaine will receive you now, Miss. I'll show your abigail her quarters and see that your trunks are carried upstairs."

"Thank you." Maeve gave Miss Grey an encouraging smile. As she started forward, her heartbeat quickened. So much of her happiness in England would depend on how well she and her aunt got along.

Bracing herself, she stepped into the drawing room.

"Oh, goodness." A fiftyish woman dressed in a stylish burgundy gown sprang from a settee, her youthful face beaming. "You're the picture of my poor late brother, only your hair and eyes are considerably lighter. Do come in, my dear."

The woman's sandy curls and sea green eyes matched Maeve's father's coloring exactly, and her features were a more delicate version of his. Seeing his flesh and blood alive again in her aunt was almost like having part of him back.

Swallowing against a tightening in her throat, she attempted the curtsy she'd practiced under Lord Faraday's tutelage. "How do you do, Lady Blaine?"

"Pray call me Aunt Eleanor." She stepped forward and took Maeve's hands. "Welcome to your new home, love. I'm so pleased to have you."

Maeve felt her eyes fill as her worries about getting along with the countess melted. "Thank you, Aunt Eleanor."

"Come and meet my dearest friend." Her aunt put an arm around her shoulders and drew her farther into the room, where she addressed a woman who was still seated. "Jane, allow me to present my niece, Miss Maeve Irvine, the one I've been telling you about for months."

Adorned in canary yellow with a matching Prussian helmet cap that covered most of her graying auburn hair, the other woman remained in her chair. She appraised Maeve with cool reserve. "Hello, Miss Irvine."

"Maeve," her aunt continued, "this is Jane Heywood, the Dowager Duchess of Ashton. Jane is little Eliza's other grandmama. Her son Adrian was married to my poor Belinda."

Though Aunt Eleanor showed no discomposure in mentioning her deceased daughter, Maeve felt a stab of grief for the cousin she'd never met. She gave her aunt a sympathetic smile. Belinda, only slightly older than Maeve herself, had made her brilliant match her first Season out, only to succumb to childbed fever two years into the marriage, after delivering her daughter Elizabeth.

She looked back to the regal figure who had been her cousin's mother-in-law. Unnerved as she felt under the woman's scrutiny, she could only imagine what trepidation Belinda must have suffered in her presence. Maeve curtsied again, hoping her performance was up to snuff for so grand a title. "Pleased to meet you, my lady."

"That is 'your grace,' Miss Irvine." The duchess affected a slight smile, but the expression didn't reach her eyes. "One addresses a duke or duchess as 'your grace.' "

Here was the aristocratic hauteur Maeve had feared to find in her aunt. Mirroring the woman's scant smile, she said, "Pray pardon me, your grace."

Aunt Eleanor gave her niece's shoulders a squeeze before removing her arm. "Don't worry, love, the basics of addressing the nobility will come to you soon—though even I have trouble with some of the more obscure rules. One cannot expect an American to catch on immediately, can one, Jane?"

Her friend lifted a hand to examine her fingernails. "I should think not."

Maeve gathered that *her grace* expected little from Americans. The woman struck her as rather disagreeable, but her aunt had described her as a great friend. She tried to give the duchess the benefit of the doubt.

"Have a seat, dear." Aunt Eleanor led her to the settee. As they sat down together, she tugged on the bellpull. "We'll have tea for you in no time. Meanwhile, tell me, was your voyage tolerable? I trust so, for your ship has docked nearly a week ahead of schedule."

"Yes, we had exceptionally good weather."

"I hope you weren't plagued with mal de mer—but from the look of you I daresay you were not. You're blooming with health."

Maeve giggled over her aunt's tendency to answer her own questions. "Thank you. I feel the best I have in over a year."

"Excellent. I confess I've spent the last month fretting over everything from stormy seas to a lack of proper company for you on the ship."

"I tried to reassure your aunt," the duchess said, "but was scarcely up to the task. Both of us were shocked to learn that your godmother declined to accompany you to England. For a young woman to undertake such a voyage without a guardian is perilous."

"My godmama still has children at home who need her care. A grown woman can travel well enough with only a maid to attend her, provided she bring along good reading material. In my case, my sketchbook served as a pastime, too."

The duchess raised an eyebrow. "Your maid must be uncommonly agreeable. I could hardly bear to spend a *day* in the company of mine."

At that moment a young woman carrying a tea tray entered the room. Maeve frowned at the duchess's careless remark, hoping the servant hadn't heard it. Expressionless, the maid placed the tray on a low table in front of her mistress.

Aunt Eleanor dismissed her and took up the silver server to pour. "La, Jane. I shouldn't mind traveling with Jones, my housekeeper. She and I have our share of comfortable little chats—though I suppose taking a transatlantic voyage together might test our patience with each other. Confining one's social contact to any single acquaintance for a month must be a trial."

The duchess accepted a cup of tea from her, then looked back to Maeve. "I don't suppose there could have been many other passengers aboard worth knowing."

"Everyone we met treated us with kindness."

"You would have done well to keep to yourselves in such a situation," she said. "A woman traveling without a male relative can easily fall prey to disreputable characters."

Maeve thought of the man on the dock and felt a

twinge of conscience. His twinkling eyes and open manner had made him seem harmless enough, but looks could be deceiving, as Miss Grey had spent a half hour reminding her afterward. In the future, she would have to behave with more reserve in public. She hated to think what Aunt Eleanor would have said if she'd known how her niece had dallied with a total stranger. Grey had gone so far as to call it flirting. Maeve hadn't intended to flirt, but perhaps *he* had seen her behavior in the same light as the abigail.

"Really, Jane, she had Captain Singer to protect her from undesirables. The man was a friend of my brother's." The countess turned to Maeve and passed her a cup and saucer. "Tell me, dear, did you meet any eligible bachelors on the way?"

"On the way?" Once more, the man at the dock came to mind. For an instant she thought her aunt must be clairvoyant. Then she realized her mistake. "Oh, on the ship, you mean? No, of course not. That is, you know I'm not looking for a husband. I came to London only to meet you, to pursue my art studies, and to try to make a name for myself as portrait painter."

"Er, yes." The countess looked down into her tea.

Maeve was sorry to see that her aunt felt uncomfortable prevaricating on her behalf, but she had no choice but to hide her wealth. She wasn't about to open herself up to fortune hunters again.

"Surely you could find a husband." The duchess sipped her tea. "Even if you're somewhat out of pocket and past your first bloom of youth, you're a handsome enough gel. You'd do very well for a country squire of modest fortune."

"She could do far better than that." Aunt Eleanor looked to Maeve. "With your beauty alone, you could have your choice of this year's crop of bachelors."

"Thank you, Aunt, but I must be realistic—"

"In person you're even lovelier than in the portrait you sent me." She leaned over the arm of the settee and picked up a miniature painting from a side table. Maeve had done the work herself half a year ago and sent it at her aunt's request. "For weeks I carried this in my reticule and boasted about you to all of my acquaintances. Did I not, Jane?"

"You did, indeed. However, you must be careful not puff up Miss Irvine's head. She's wise to be practical." The duchess turned to Maeve. "You could certainly make a respectable match, dear, but don't let your aunt persuade you to shoot for the stars. The top bachelors here will be seeking more than just a comely face."

Maeve opened her mouth to protest being described as such, but, for her aunt's sake, she snapped her jaw shut again. A hot surge of annoyance crept up the back of her neck. She took great pride in her accomplishments and little pleasure in her looks.

"I'll have you know that Maeve is highly accomplished," Aunt Eleanor said in a firm voice. "She was among the first females elected to the Boston Academy of Fine Arts. And if it's her breeding you're questioning, I'll remind you that my niece is the granddaughter of an earl."

"But she's also an . . ." Her friend stopped and cleared her throat. "Eleanor, you know very well that our titled men want a financially advantageous match."

"Then they must be surprisingly like American men," Maeve said, suspecting that her nationality comprised the woman's unspoken objection. "Still, none of this matters. My dream is to become an eminent portrait painter, not to make a magnificent marriage."

Her aunt placed the miniature back down on the

table. "I'm sure you can do whatever you put your mind to, love."

The sound of a carriage slowing out front made everyone look up, but the street lay too far below the window to see.

"That will be Adrian, at last." The duchess set down her tea. "His errands took him longer than he estimated. He was supposed to collect Eliza and me an hour ago."

"I'm glad he's running late, or you would have missed Maeve's arrival." Aunt Eleanor looked toward the main hall as a knock came at the front door. "How fortunate that you chose not to bring your own barouche today. Now Maeve has the opportunity to meet Adrian, too."

"Yes, how fortunate."

The duchess's tone failed to convey pleasure, and Maeve concluded that she didn't deem a lowly American important enough to meet her son. Frankly, Maeve would have as lief passed on the acquaintance, anyway. The man was likely as disagreeable as his mother.

The butler ducked into the room and announced the duke. Behind him a tall man entered in the midst of taking off a hat. He swept his thick, dark hair out of his eyes, and Maeve got her first full view of his face—one she recognized.

It was the man she'd met at the London wharf.

Her jaw dropped. Good Lord, she'd been flirting with the Duke of Ashton, her own cousin's husband! Even harder to credit, that playful rogue was the son of the overbearing duchess.

"Good day, Lady Blaine," he said to her aunt before Maeve's gawking drew his notice. When he met her gaze, his eyes widened and the smile fled his face.

Her heart skipped a beat. She didn't know what to expect next. She gulped and waited for him to react, half expecting him to continue the banter they'd exchanged earlier. In this setting such behavior would look impertinent. They would have to explain their prior meeting to the others present, and the story would make her look very forward indeed.

"I'm glad you dropped by today," Aunt Eleanor said, drawing his attention back to her.

He bowed to her, then to the group in general. The color began to return to his face.

While his mother greeted him, Maeve struggled to regain her composure. Unfortunately, her nerves were shattered. Her kind aunt would be mortified when the duke told everyone how she had comported herself. She would be lucky if she still had a place to stay tonight.

Tears stung her eyes, and she blinked rapidly to try to keep them from overflowing. The prospect of living with family again had been such a comfort to her. Now she feared she'd ruined her relationship with the one close relative she had left, all for a few minutes of dalliance. Once again, her fascination with a man had led her to make a disastrous decision.

"If I'm not mistaken, Lady Blaine, I must request the pleasure of meeting your niece." The duke gave Maeve a sober look. "I believe I recognize this lady from a miniature you've shown me."

So that was why he'd believed he knew her when they'd met. She stared at him, her thoughts a jumble.

"Yes, I was just telling Maeve how disgracefully I've boasted of her beauty." Rising, Lady Blaine reached out to her and urged her to her feet.

She got up slowly, horrified that her brazen behavior would now be exposed to her aunt—not to mention the haughty duchess. If the latter had only suspected her of being an ill-bred hoyden before, this would solidify her opinion.

Aunt Eleanor performed the formal introductions, and Maeve summoned all of her will to give the man a weak smile.

He answered her expression with a grimace. “Oddly enough, I feel as though I know you already.”

She lowered her gaze, prepared for the storm.

“Oh, dear, have I told you *that* much about my niece?” her aunt asked, saving her for the time being.

“Only a detail or two.”

“You know, then, that Maeve has lived in America all of her life but plans to settle in England now that her father and mother are both gone.”

A moment of silence hovered heavily in the air. At last Maeve looked up and saw the duke watching her with softened eyes.

“I’m sorry, Miss Irvine. I had forgotten your history. Please accept my condolences.”

“Thank you,” she said, surprised by the sympathy she read in his face. She supposed that, having lost a wife, he knew grief only too well. Quietly, she added, “Papa’s been gone for more than a year, however, and Mama much longer. I still miss them very much, but when I decided to move here, I resolved to be done with melancholy.”

He gave her a long, unreadable look.

“Eliza is down for a nap,” his mother said, breaking the spell. “Will you go and collect her, Adrian?”

“Let me ring for Jones.” Aunt Eleanor reached for the bell.

The duke held up a hand. “No, no. I’ll fetch the baby. I may be able to get her without waking her.”

She smiled. “Of course. That would be best.”

He started to walk away, but his mother called after him. “Why were you late today, Adrian? Did you run into trouble at the docks?”

The tension in Maeve's body tightened.

He glanced back at her, then met his mother's gaze. "None worth mentioning. The shipment is safely off."

Turning again, he left the room.

Maeve watched until he vanished into the hall. Was that all, then? Wasn't he going to divulge her frivolity? He had passed up the perfect opportunity. Could she possibly be in the clear?

Her aunt returned to the settee and asked the duchess something. Maeve's brain was too addled to follow the conversation.

She sat down in a daze. What had kept the man silent about her social gaffe? Was he protecting her? Did his own behavior at the docks embarrass him? Perhaps he didn't want his meddlesome mother digging into every detail of their encounter.

Whatever the case, she owed him her gratitude.

"You look somewhat peaked, dear." Her aunt's voice broke into her thoughts. "I fear your journey is catching up with you. Perhaps I should have Jones show you your chamber."

Maeve tried to smile. "I confess that I could use a few minutes to refresh myself."

Her aunt rang for the housekeeper, who arrived almost immediately.

As Maeve followed Mrs. Jones upstairs, her nerves began to subside. The more she thought about the duke, the more she appreciated his discretion. Keeping quiet had unquestionably benefited her more than him. Despite his haughty mother, his elevated title, and his good looks, he seemed quite capable of empathy. It was easy to see why Belinda had fallen for him.

A sigh escaped her, and she noticed it sounded wistful.

*Goose,* she admonished herself. Some women made

auspicious marriages; others—such as she—were destined to find fulfillment elsewhere. To preserve her chances for happiness, she would do well to remember that.

Adrian ran up the stairs, unconsciously duplicating with his body the speed of his racing thoughts. He could scarcely believe that the blonde from the docks had turned out to be Belinda's cousin. The one woman who'd managed to lift the cloud of bitterness hanging around him was related to the one who had spurred his misery. Fate loved to play practical jokes.

He couldn't deny that he was disappointed.

Reaching the second floor, he turned up the hall, replaying in his mind the moment of his disillusion. Maeve Irvine's connection to his wife had staggered him so much he hadn't known whether or not to acknowledge their earlier meeting. Why had he kept it to himself? If he hadn't, his mother and mother-in-law would have condemned Miss Irvine's behavior at the docks, but why should *he* have bothered to protect the little minx from their disapproval?

Only one reason came to mind: Part of him still craved more of the saucy treatment that he had kept a secret.

He was a fool.

Outside of the nursery he paused to collect himself. It wouldn't do to burst in and wake Eliza, possibly even alarm her if she sensed his agitation.

He took several deep breaths, then gently opened the door. The drawn drapes made the room too dark to enter. While his eyes adjusted, he listened to the baby's quiet, regular breathing. She was still asleep.

Slowly the furnishings came into view. He left the

door ajar and crept across the bare floorboards. At the crib he gazed down at Eliza's soft, round face, and his chest constricted. Belinda had claimed she didn't know whether or not he was the child's sire, and nothing about Eliza's looks told him she was his . . . nor any other man's. With her tawny curls and delicate features, she distinctly took after her mother.

He reached under the toddler's arms and lifted her to his chest. She stirred and settled against his shoulder. The heat of life flowing through her, her pliancy, her smallness, all made him keenly aware of her total dependence on him. He loved her more than anything else, and the possibility that she might not be his only made him more fiercely protective. It was as though she'd been dealt an unfair blow right at her conception. He wanted to make amends to her by ensuring that everything else in her life went right.

After all, the blame for the question surrounding her birth lay partly at his feet. Had he known how to make Belinda happy, she never would have turned to another lover.

For several moments he stood in the darkness, taking comfort in the warmth of his daughter. The rocking chair by the crib tempted him to sit and stay upstairs. He didn't want to return to his mother's habitual questioning and advice, nor to Maeve Irvine's big eyes fixed upon him. The woman had looked chagrined about his arrival. Apparently, she regretted the way she'd behaved at the docks—but why? Likely only because he now knew who she was. Now he might tell her aunt and others how brazen she could be.

Exactly how brazen was that? He frowned. She was Belinda's cousin. Perhaps a lack of virtue ran in the family. Who knew how far Miss Irvine's flirtations might go?

The sound of voices in the hall prompted him to look over his shoulder. Though the door stood open, he couldn't see around it from his position. Soft feminine murmurings grazed his ears, but he couldn't make out the words. At first he thought the ladies had come upstairs in search of him, but no one entered the nursery. Somewhere nearby, a door closed, and one set of footsteps faded down the hall. The other went silent.

*I'd better go down before they do come,* he thought. *The best thing I can do is go home.* Gathering Eliza close to him, he turned to leave the room.

As he stepped outside, the door across the hall opened. Maeve Irvine popped her head out, looking down the empty corridor and calling, "Mrs. Jones?"

Instantly she sensed his presence, and her gaze shot to meet his. She started. "Oh. Your grace."

Looking down at Eliza, he twirled a finger in her gossamer hair. "Miss Irvine."

For a moment neither of them spoke. Then her skirts rustled as she stepped into the hallway.

"This is your daughter?" she asked softly. "My second cousin?"

He nodded and looked at her.

A faint smile grazed her lips, and her eyes looked watery. "She's beautiful."

Surely she couldn't be crying. Why would she? He cleared his throat. "Eliza is fortunate in that she favors her mother."

"But her hair has a hint of red in it, I think." She moved closer, her smile widening. "That comes from your side. Your mother has auburn hair."

Surprised, he glanced back down at the baby. Sparks of sunlight reflected off a chandelier above the staircase, and the highlights they ignited in her hair did appear to have a strawberry tint. But, no, he refused to succumb to false hopes. "I would call Eliza's hair tawny."

Another stretch of silence passed while Miss Irvine gazed at the baby. Finally she looked up at him. "Thank you for keeping quiet about our meeting at the docks."

"Why should my silence matter?"

She drew in a breath. "My manners must have seemed rather, er . . . forward. Aunt Eleanor knows me only through correspondence, and I would hate for her to suspect me ill-bred before we've even had a chance to get acquainted. I hope *you* won't judge me too harshly, either, your grace."

"I'm not accustomed to such familiar treatment from a stranger." *From anyone, really,* he thought. A lofty title like his didn't encourage familiarity in general.

"Of course not, and I apologize." She held his gaze with a steadiness that suggested sincerity. "I'm not usually so forward. My spirits were high in anticipation of starting a new life in England. 'Tis no excuse, but I simply got carried away."

Studying her, he twisted his mouth. She had an openness unlike that of the British women he knew, and her candor swayed him. Had her deportment at the docks truly been so dreadful? It was hard to argue that she had behaved any worse than he. At the time he might have believed he'd known her, but in fact he hadn't. "I daresay I was carried away, too."

She broke into an ingenuous grin. "Suppose we start our acquaintance over? This time I'll afford you all of the respect my cousin's widower deserves."

Her smile charmed him, but it also reminded him that he had a weakness for her. He paused but eventually nodded. "And I'll afford you the respect *you* deserve."

His hesitation and grim tone seemed to underscore

the ambiguity of his words. A question hung between them: How much respect *did* she deserve?

Her smile faded, but he chose not to amend his statement. The most he could have assured her was that for now he would reserve judgment.

Nonetheless, the ensuing lapse in conversation made him worry that he'd ventured too close to insulting her. Their encounter at the docks flashed in his mind. Upon meeting, they had seemed to have an immediate rapport. When they'd parted, he had practically begged to see her again. If he alienated her now, would he come to regret it? He wasn't sure what he wanted from her—a flirtation, a courtship—but for now, he didn't want to close any doors.

He moistened his lips and mustered up a lighter tone. "So what time shall I stop by tomorrow?"

Confusion flickered through her features. Her brows drew together. "Pardon?"

Her obvious bewilderment teased a crooked smile to his lips. "You don't remember? I promised to call on you, if it was at all in my power."

Her eyes rounded. Then she laughed, that throaty chuckle that had warmed his soul earlier. "I could not hold you to a promise made under such circumstances."

He shook his head. "I keep my vows, Miss Irvine."

She raised an eyebrow but nodded, as if surprised by his preaching but amenable to his principles. "Commendable of you. Well, I don't know what my aunt's schedule for tomorrow holds, but if she has nothing else in mind for me, you may call anytime you like."

"I'll confer with Lady Blaine on my way out. Unless she has other plans, I'll see you at ten." He bowed as well as he could with Eliza in his arms. "Welcome to England."

"Thank you."

He started to walk away, then paused to look over his shoulder at her. "Shall I send Mrs. Jones to you?"

She still stood in the same spot where he had left her. "Yes, please, if it's not too much trouble."

Turning around again, he walked to the stairs. He listened to the shuffle of footsteps and the sound of her chamber door closing. When he knew he was out of her sight, his shoulders relaxed. Until that moment, he hadn't realized how tense he'd been. Was he mad to keep this mockery of a promise to call on her tomorrow? Would doing so only be furthering a flirtation they had started at the docks? Was his talk about keeping vows merely an excuse?

He took the stairs at a much slower pace than he had when he'd ascended. Miss Irvine undeniably still appealed to him—rather too much for his comfort. He had to avoid falling into flirtation with her, at least until he learned more about her character. Doing so might not prove easy, after the precedent they'd set at their first meeting, but the last thing he needed was another Belinda to lure him in . . . and break him.

Reaching the bottom of the stairs, he steeled his jaw. Surely he was overreacting to a little bit of playfulness. Even if Miss Irvine turned out to be just as treacherous as Belinda, he was older now and not so impetuous as he'd been when he had married. He had learned his lesson. Women like Belinda and her minx of a cousin held no power over him.

He'd do well to keep that in mind when he returned to see Miss Irvine in the morning.

# Three

Maeve spent the afternoon unpacking, then passed a long and enjoyable evening getting better acquainted with her aunt. The women chatted nonstop until midnight. Even then, Maeve retired with reluctance, but after such a full day she slept straight through the night.

Miss Grey woke her at a decent hour the next morning—fortunately, for she didn't want to look like a slugabed. The abigail differed with her over how lavishly she ought to dress, but since Maeve owned the clothes and the body on which they went, her opinion prevailed. She went down to breakfast in the simple lavender frock she had chosen from the start.

Following the mouthwatering aroma of cooking bacon, she arrived at the dining room at nine. While she stood at the sideboard selecting an egg and toast, her aunt joined her.

The countess placed a crescent roll on her plate, then stifled a yawn. "Goodness, we stayed up late last night. When I awoke this morning, I could barely drag myself out of bed."

"I'm sorry. I shouldn't have pressed you to tell me so many stories about my father."

"Indeed?" Her aunt laughed. "I thought *I* had insisted on telling them."

"Not at all." Maeve carried her food to the table and

chose a seat. "It's been some time since anyone has told me anything new of my father. I could have sat up listening for half the night."

"In that case, I wish I could have appeased you, but perhaps it's just as well we retired when we did." Aunt Eleanor sat down across from her and opened her napkin. "I just remembered that Adrian said he would come by this morning. Did I mention that to you last night?"

"No, but *he* told me."

"He did?" Her aunt looked at her, setting down the butter knife she'd just picked up.

Her evident surprise made Maeve wish the subject hadn't come up. Though she felt closer to the countess than she had on first arriving, she still didn't dare explain how the duke's promise had originated. She could only hope that someday she'd be comfortable enough to confess all, and the two of them would share a laugh over the story.

She made a show of pouring two cups of tea and steeled herself to the guilt of holding back the full truth. "I ran into him after Mrs. Jones first showed me to my chamber. He was coming out of the nursery with Eliza."

"And he told you he would call this morning?"

Maeve squirmed under her scrutiny, aware that it sounded as though the duke were more interested in her than he was. She longed to blurt out everything, but the risk of disapproval was too great.

She seized her spoon and used an inordinate amount of concentration to stir her cup. "Considerate of him, isn't it? He seems to want me to feel welcomed."

" 'Tis very unusual. Adrian doesn't often make much effort socially." Aunt Eleanor lifted her knife again and took a pat of butter. "He was in a curious humor yesterday. Even when I introduced you, I thought he acted oddly . . . cordial but somehow insinuating."

"Indeed?" Maeve forced herself to meet her aunt's gaze briefly before looking down to sip her tea.

"Perhaps I misinterpreted a mere personality quirk. Now that I know he made a point of promising *you* to call today, it occurs to me he must have acted the way he did because he was so struck by your beauty. I want you to know that I have no absurd idea of his belonging to Belinda. If the two of you could find happiness together, nothing would please me more."

Maeve nearly spit out a mouthful of tea. For a moment she couldn't respond. She hoped her aunt didn't sense her *slight* attraction to the duke and get the idea that she meant to pursue him. Unfortunately, this fear would only add to her need to conceal how she'd behaved at the dock.

"There's no question he's noticed your looks," the countess said. "He actually recognized you from your portrait! For him to promise to call today, you must have made quite an impression. It would be marvelous if you two made a match."

"It would be a marvel, certainly," Maeve finally choked out. "Urbane dukes do not marry silly American girls."

"You're not silly. You are a lovely, well-mannered woman—and I've never known Adrian to pay heed to status, if that's what you're thinking. He won't care that you're American, that you have no title, or even that you apparently must paint to make a living."

Maeve pursed her lips. "I'd wager his mother would care."

"Ah, you sensed Jane's prejudice against Americans." She looked down at her plate. "I must apologize for her. She lost a brother in your war for independence, so the States are not her favorite country. But she'll soon come to love you as I already do. In any case, her opinion has no bearing on Adrian's decisions."

Maeve could scarcely believe they were entertaining such a preposterous discussion. "I must remind you that I'm not seeking a husband."

"But you never know what might happen, dear. For little Eliza to have you, her own second cousin, stand in for her mother would be the most natural thing in the world."

When she opened her mouth to protest again, she met a gaze so full of hope and affection that she stopped herself and sighed. Let her aunt hold onto her little fantasy for the time being. Soon enough, she would come to see that Maeve had no desire to marry.

She forced a smile and set her mind to steering the conversation elsewhere. "Eliza is beautiful, by the way. She takes after her mother, judging by Belinda's portraits."

"Do you think so? As a newborn, she reminded me very much of Belinda, but I believe she's beginning to look more like Adrian as she grows." Aunt Eleanor bit into her roll.

They spent the rest of breakfast discussing Eliza's development. Maeve was amused by tales of the child's first successes at speech and looked forward to getting to know her.

When they'd both finished eating, the countess set down her napkin and rose. "If you'll excuse me, I have a few matters to discuss with Jones before Adrian arrives. I'll join you in the drawing room shortly."

"Thank you." Maeve stood, too. "I believe I'll fetch my sketchbook and draw while I wait."

On the way to her chamber, she reflected on the wild twist their conversation had taken earlier. Was it at all possible the duke was interested in her? He'd definitely been attentive at the docks, but that was before he'd realized who she was. Even if he had been attracted then, her relationship to his wife likely changed everything. Surely the reminder of Belinda would be too much to overcome.

*And what does it matter to me anyway?* she thought as she reached her room. Her days of pursuing men were over. She had best make sure that the duke's feelings for her *didn't* matter, or she'd be setting herself up for another disappointment.

Opening the door, she found Miss Grey unpacking one of the trunks they hadn't gotten to the previous day.

The abigail heard her enter and looked up from her work. "Oh, thank heavens. You've changed your mind about what you're wearing."

"Indeed, I have not." Maeve crossed the room to the desk. "I merely came to fetch my sketchbook."

"Oh, please, Miss. That frock isn't suitable for receiving a duke. You are no longer in half mourning." She leaned over the trunk and pulled out a gold-and-white striped gown with a matching spencer. "How about this one? I can have it pressed in a trice."

"Too extravagant." Maeve shuffled through the clutter on the desk and pulled out her book. "Remember that I'm supposed to be in financial straits now."

"But a duke is coming to visit you. Surely you don't fear that *he* is a fortune hunter."

"It doesn't matter. He's a lofty British aristocrat, he's my cousin's widower, and I've made a mortifying social gaffe in front of him. Any kindness he shows me is what he would show any minor relative." She opened a drawer and searched for a soft-leaded pencil. "I'm not changing my plan. As far as anyone is concerned, I'm a woman who paints portraits for a living."

"But must you wear the shabbiest dress you own," the

abigail asked in a wheedling tone, "when you're expecting such a grand visitor?"

Maeve turned around to face her, putting her free hand on her hip. "I thought you didn't like the duke."

"I didn't like you speaking to a man you didn't know." She tilted her head to the side. "Now that you've been properly introduced, it's another story."

"My story hasn't changed one whit." Maeve drew her book to her chest and walked toward the door. "You and I needn't come out and lie about my situation, but we do need to let on that I'm here because I have to be, and clothing makes a significant impression."

Miss Grey's shoulders sagged. She mumbled, "Yes, Miss."

Maeve shook her head to herself. Her own confused feelings for the duke were vexing enough without everyone around urging her to pursue him. Attempting to keep her spirits high, she said over her shoulder, "Try repeating this to yourself: *We're here for the money. We're here for the money.*"

Miss Grey gave her a look of utter disapproval.

Suddenly the absurdity of the situation struck Maeve, and she laughed out loud. "Such a Friday face! Grey, I think that over the last day I've faced more censure from you than previously in my entire adult life."

The abigail pursed her lips and turned back to unpacking the trunk. "You're rather lively for a woman in dire straits, Miss. You'd best heed your own advice and take care not to give yourself away."

Adrian drove his curricle to Lady Blaine's house in unusually high spirits. He supposed the beautiful late spring weather must have lifted his mood. The sun shone brilliantly in a clear blue sky, and a temperate breeze carried the scent of blooming tulips from the cart of a passing street vendor. Amazing how awakening from the barren cold of winter gave one such a sense of renewed life each year. It was as if the strengthening sunlight accelerated one's vigor.

The fact that he had managed to avoid a plethora of questions from his mother also helped, he realized, leaning in as the phaeton rounded a bend. The duchess insisted on knowing every detail of his life. Whenever they stayed in the country, she lived down the drive in the dowager house, but here they resided under a single roof. The difference her presence made in his freedom astonished him. In the future, he would have to think twice before coming to town at the same time as she. Fortunately, this morning she had taken Eliza to the park. As soon as they'd disappeared down the street with a groom, Adrian had slipped away.

He guided the horses onto Lady Blaine's street, and his blood quickened. *That* had nothing to do with the season, he conceded. The prospect of seeing Miss Irvine excited him, whether wise or not. To own up to the truth, he couldn't wait to further their acquaintance and see if his attraction to her still held fast.

For the hundredth time in the last twenty-four hours, the few encounters they'd had flashed through his mind. She didn't seem like a self-centered child, as Belinda often had. He had noted how Miss Irvine's eyes filled with tears so readily. The woman clearly knew grief, yet she was determined to recover and move on. He could learn a lesson from her. For too many years, he had wallowed in bitterness.

When he arrived at the house, the butler led him to the drawing room. Pausing in the doorway, Adrian observed Miss Irvine on the settee with a large leatherbound book propped on her lap. As she studied the volume, a tiny crease puckered her brow. She definitely had a pensive vein in her character that her late cousin had lacked.

"The Duke of Ashton," the butler announced in a booming voice.

Miss Irvine started, her reverie interrupted. She snapped the book shut and sprang to her feet.

While they exchanged greetings, he observed how guileless she looked in the simply styled frock she wore. To think that only yesterday he'd speculated that she might be someone's mistress! He couldn't have dreamed up a more absurd notion. Would that more women of the gentry dressed as modestly as she and allowed their natural beauty to speak for itself.

"Reading Shakespeare again?" he asked as they sat down facing each other. Perhaps referring to their first meeting was indiscreet of him. His manner, he noticed, seemed rather familiar. Somehow, he felt as though he knew her more intimately than he actually did.

"Not this time." She smiled but lowered her gaze and set the book on a table beside her. "I was just sketching."

"Ah, yes, I recall hearing that you're a serious artist." Interested, he leaned forward in his chair. Here was a chance to peek into her personality. "Will you show me your drawings?"

"Oh—I'd rather not." She put her hand over the cover of the book. "They're, er . . . personal. Perhaps another time."

Her apparent embarrassment tempted him to tease her. He cocked an eyebrow. "What could you possibly be sketching that you'd find necessary to hide?"

She looked up at him with wide eyes.

He hadn't meant for his comment to sound suggestive, but her expression of shock made him grin. "I mean, given your reputed artistic talent, you have no reason to be shy about your work."

She gazed at him for another moment, then gave him a faint smile and shook her head. "I'm afraid there's nothing in here so intriguing as you imagine."

"Perhaps you overrate my imagination."

She laughed. "I daresay you have a lively imagination."

The remark surprised him. For years he'd found nothing about himself lively. Hadn't he been so tediously stolid that he'd driven Belinda into the bed of another man? He leaned on the arm of his chair. "What makes you say so?"

"Well, yesterday you imagined that you knew me." She gave him a grin that made her eyes sparkle. "That took some creative thinking. Now you're implying that I'm concealing a sketchbook full of anatomy studies, are you not?"

It was his turn to gape. In truth, such a thought had crossed his mind, but to voice it certainly had not. He wondered if speaking so freely was a trait typical of Americans or peculiar to her.

"As you remarked, I *am* a serious artist," she went on when he didn't respond, "but, to appease your curiosity, the Boston Academy of the Fine Arts does not furnish its students with nude models."

The subject matter she broached astounded him, but he had to admit he'd never before known a woman who had formally studied art. Perhaps among her fellow students no one raised an eyebrow over a discussion of anatomy studies in mixed company.

He began to wonder about her education. Exactly how much *had* the Academy taught her about anatomy? Nude models or not, as an artist she doubtlessly knew more about the human form than most women of his acquaintance—and many of the men, too. The chap who married her would likely not have to worry about a turbulent wedding night.

The notion drew his gaze downward to her pert breasts before he could wrench it back to her face.

Luckily, she had turned back to her sketchbook. She picked up the volume and flipped through the pages. "To stem your wild imaginings, I will show you the drawing I was working on—but if you find it a poor likeness, you must remember that I haven't yet had adequate time to study the subject."

Getting up, she walked over and stood next to him. She leaned forward, and her arm brushed his shoulder. His skin tingled with the warmth of her touch. A lock of her hair had escaped its bun and hung near his face. The faint fragrance of rosewater grazed his nose.

With effort, he fixed his attention on the book she held in front of him. On the page, he recognized the image of his daughter.

"It's Eliza," he murmured in surprise.

In sweeping pencil strokes, Miss Irvine had faithfully captured the contours of the sleeping baby's face. She had mastered Eliza's small upturned nose, and the curve of the cheek was unmistakable. The familiar long-lashed eyes tugged at his heart, just as the original ones did.

He smiled. "The likeness is amazing."

"Well, don't examine the details too closely. I'm sure I've misrepresented some of her features." She closed the book and took it back to the settee with her. "Some time when I have her present, I'll do a better one."

He longed to admire the sketch further, but she plainly feared it didn't represent her best work. Instead of pressing her, he said, "I've never had Eliza's likeness taken. You make me realize that I should. Already she's growing into a toddler. She won't be a baby much longer."

"When I do a proper sketch of her, you can have it."

Her generosity took him aback. He shook his head. "Oh, no, I couldn't ask you to forfeit the product of your labors."

" 'Tis no great imposition." She gave him an impish smile. "Perhaps you'll like my work and commission me to do a complete painting."

Lady Blaine appeared at that moment, and he rose. While they exchanged pleasantries, he wondered about Miss Irvine's last comment. The previous night his mother had remarked to him that the young American had a distasteful bent for commercial painting. He supposed Miss Irvine must not be well off—certainly her clothes weren't very fine—but resorting to trade did seem somewhat desperate. No well-bred Englishwoman he knew would stoop to painting for money. Perhaps Miss Irvine believed that a woman without a dowry had little chance of finding a husband.

A quick mental inventory of his bachelor friends and their financial expectations caused him to frown.

Perhaps she was right.

She opened her sketchbook again to show Lady Blaine the drawing of Eliza. Adrian stepped forward and took a second look, the fresh smell of Miss Irvine's hair again tantalizing him. While the ladies conversed, he considered how different she was from other women he knew. Was his mother correct to suggest she was ill-bred? At one time he would have thought so, but he'd married a "well-bred" female and found that Belinda's gentility had borne little relevance to her character. Miss Irvine was the product of a foreign culture. She had undertaken ventures he'd never imagined a female attempting.

For now he would withhold judgment.

"Where is your mother today?" Lady Blaine asked him as everyone sat. "I'd hoped she might tag along with you."

"She took Eliza to the park."

The countess glanced at Miss Irvine, then looked back to him. "She's been going to the park quite frequently this year. I don't recall her enjoying walking so much in past Seasons."

He thought about it and acknowledged that the duchess had been out in the air rather often lately. Perhaps she, too, found their living arrangements confining. He shrugged off the idea. "I'm glad to see her taking an interest in her health."

"I'm not convinced that her health is what interests her." Lady Blaine frowned. "Do you suppose she has a beau she is pursuing?"

A laugh escaped him. "After ten years as a widow? I hardly think so. More likely, she wants some time away from me."

His hostess said nothing more, but for another moment she appeared oddly thoughtful.

The three of them spent another quarter hour chatting, the women regaling him with family stories they'd dug from their memories the previous evening. Aunt and niece had clearly found plenty of common ground already, occasionally even finishing each other's sentences. He enjoyed the conversation, but he soon realized he'd stayed past the time of a polite visit. Reluctantly, he rose and bid the ladies farewell.

As he left the house and walked toward his curricle, Lady Blaine appeared at the door and called after him.

He retraced his path to the bottom of the front steps and looked up at her. "Yes, my lady?"

"I'm sorry to detain you. I just wondered if you knew

whether Jane plans to go to Lady Postlethwaite's musical evening tonight."

He knew only too well. For days his mother had been hounding him to attend with her and meet a debutante she hoped he would like. He'd told her he had no further interest in taking that route, but she didn't take him seriously, not knowing his reasons. He'd already married the most sparkling debutante of one Season, and the experience had poisoned his life.

"Indeed she does," he said.

"Oh, good. We're going, too. I thought a musicale might be a good first outing for Maeve—not too socially demanding."

*Nor too interesting,* he thought, though he nodded as if in agreement.

"Will you be there?" She studied him closely. "I'm sure Maeve would appreciate having a few familiar faces present for her first appearance among the London *ton.*"

He hesitated. The gathering promised to be a bore, but he sympathized with Miss Irvine's being cast among several of the cattiest matrons in Society. The chit's unconventional ways could easily draw out a number of extended claws. Perhaps he could spare her some grief by deflecting some of the questions away from her.

"Yes, I'll go," he said, a bit stunned by his own decision.

His mother-in-law broke into a wide grin. "Excellent. Then we'll see you there tonight."

The countess returned to the house, and he started back toward his curricle again. He wondered whether he'd been daft to agree to her request. Lady Blaine certainly seemed concerned about her niece. Obviously, *she* didn't find Miss Irvine's eccentricities beyond the pale. Then again, she didn't know about the saucy smiles at the dock . . . and, likely, her niece didn't speak of anatomy studies to her.

Or did she? He didn't know exactly how eccentric Miss Irvine might be. Her unpredictability intrigued him—and concerned him. Whether the sense of unease he felt was for her or himself, he wasn't quite sure.

The sound of feminine voices from above made him glance upward. He spotted Miss Irvine standing near a second-story window, her back turned toward him.

With no thought to his actions, he stopped and gazed up, admiring the soft curve of her shoulder.

"I don't care if it's seemly or not, Grey," she said to someone deeper inside the room.

Grey was her abigail, he remembered from the docks, the matron who had admonished Miss Irvine against speaking to a stranger. If the maid spent her days trying to rein in her mistress, she had her work cut out for her. He wondered what the woman was denouncing now but couldn't make out her response.

"I told you to remember," Miss Irvine continued. *"We're here for the money."*

The blunt words startled him, and he realized he was eavesdropping. He resumed walking, but Miss Irvine had stepped away from the window anyway.

*What in blazes did she mean by that?* he pondered as he untied his horses. What money had she come to London for? As far as he knew she had only one connection here: her aunt.

A sick knot curled in his stomach. Miss Irvine must have come to weasel her way into Lady Blaine's affection—and will.

The thought disturbed him, not only because he cared about his mother-in-law—which he did—but because the countess's considerable wealth was currently willed to Eliza. As long as he could help it, nobody was going to take away *anything* that belonged to Eliza.

Frowning, he climbed up on the curricle. He realized he hadn't heard much of Miss Irvine's conversation, and he hoped there was another explanation for her comment. Could it be *his* money she'd been talking about, or the money of any man? If so, wouldn't she have said she was here to find a *husband,* like any *normal* fortune huntress? Had she been referring to a business interest? He believed Lady Blaine would have mentioned such a venture to him, as he was their closest male relative . . . but it was possible, he supposed.

He set his jaw and urged the horses on. He'd simply have to learn more, without revealing he'd overheard what he had.

Perhaps agreeing to attend Lady Postlethwaite's function had been fortuitous after all. Whatever was going on, one certainty stood out: He would have to keep a close watch on Maeve Irvine until he knew more about her.

# Four

Adrian tied his cravat before a cheval mirror in his chamber. In his reflection he noted a rare sparkle in his eye and a ruddiness to his cheeks. Was he actually excited about an event he would normally deem dull as dishwater?

Crafting a meticulous knot, he told himself he was simply eager to begin his investigation of Maeve Irvine. He'd spent all day thinking about her, alternatively worrying about her designs on Lady Blaine's fortune . . . and ruminating over her lithe figure.

He leaned closer to the glass to examine a shaving nick he'd sustained earlier. The mark was nearly undetectable, and he ended up scrutinizing his face for something else: an ulterior motive. Were his suspicions about Miss Irvine well-founded or merely based on a desire to be near her? He had to admit he rather enjoyed the idea of keeping an eye on her.

Then again, the words *we're here for the money* sounded bloody suspicious.

The thought prompted another emotion to flicker across the face in the reflection: trepidation. He really didn't *want* to find her untrustworthy.

He didn't want to be attracted to another woman like Belinda.

His toilette finished, he went to his mother's chamber

to confirm that he would escort her to the Postlethwaites'. He found her seated before her cherry wood vanity, a maid diligently pinning up her hair.

"You really are attending?" She turned partially toward him while the maid continued working. The presence of a servant never prevented the duchess from speaking with her usual freedom. "I'm so pleased. I was certain you'd renege at the last moment. Up until this morning you vowed you'd never go to another musicale after what you called 'the travesty' at the Hawkes' last year."

He shrugged. "I like music when it's well done. You've told me so much about Lady Louisa Postlethwaite's talents that you've convinced me this event will be different."

She gave him a broad smile. "Are you *interested* in the gel, Adrian? It's said that music is the 'food of love.'"

A weight seemed to fall upon him. At least a thousand times he and his mother had discussed his finding a new wife, and he still hadn't learned how to handle the topic without emotion. Of course, she didn't know quite how unpalatable he considered the idea of remarrying. Like everyone else of his acquaintance, he duchess had never learned the full story of Belinda's betrayal.

He gave her a stony stare. "Why do you persist with such unfounded conjecture, Mother? You know I have no intention of marrying again."

"I also know that you loathe musicales, so I suspect something unusual is drawing you to this one." She looked into the mirror above the vanity and twirled a curl around one well-manicured finger. "But never mind. I shall say no more. I think I've made my preferences clear already."

Yes, she certainly had made it known that Lady Louisa was her latest hope for a new daughter-in-law.

"I shan't bother arguing further, either," he said with a tight rein on his emotions. "How can I, when you refuse to take me at my word? When you're ready to leave, I'll be in my study."

His mood ruined, he stalked downstairs and poured himself a generous snifter of brandy. He downed a burning mouthful and sank into his favorite leather armchair. Though he tried to clear his mind, he couldn't block the usual rush of memories.

The anger always hit him first: outrage that Belinda had taken up with a gutless aristocratic French fugitive while he, her husband, was off in the Peninsula fighting the bastard's war for him. True to his nature, *Comte Le Coward* had fled England before Adrian got a chance to deal with him, leaving behind the beautiful, treacherous Belinda . . . with child.

He staved off a wave of nausea with another gulp of brandy. The disgust would soon pass as the guilt took over. Four seemingly endless months of ranting and sulking flashed through his head. Next had come the resentment of the unborn child, before at last he had resolved to accept the baby as his own. Then suddenly the nightmare had ended—his deceitful wife whisked away like so much bad rubbish.

For a while afterward, he'd feared that he had wished that fate upon her—but, no, he'd only wished to have back the wife he'd believed he married. For that illusory Belinda he had grieved hard. And once he'd held Eliza, he had never again felt anything but love for her.

"I'm ready, Adrian." His mother's voice preceded her knock on the open door. She poked her head into the room, and her face fell. No doubt his grim expression and the open decanter served as indicators of where his thoughts had turned, though she would assume that grief alone engulfed him.

Coming forward, she placed a hand on his shoulder. "I apologize for my thoughtless comments, Adrian."

He put his hand over hers briefly, then gently removed her fingers from his shoulder as he rose. "I know you mean well." Without meeting her gaze, he replaced the stopper in the brandy. "We had best be on our way. We wouldn't want to miss any of Lady Louisa's fine playing."

The duchess watched him in silence for a moment longer and finally nodded.

During the drive to the musicale, Adrian managed to shake off his unpleasant memories, but his mood remained dark. When they reached the Postlethwaites' town house and their hosts greeted them, he tried to affect a more suitable humor, but he doubted his forced smiles passed for genuine.

Nevertheless, Lady Blaine expressed delight in seeing him, and Miss Irvine gave him a dazzling smile that sent his heartbeat racing. Aware of her possible treachery, he kept his response aloof and offered her a halfhearted bow.

"I'm so glad you're here," she said, as their companions fell into a private conversation. "The prospect of a musical evening is lovely, but if you hadn't come, my aunt would have been my only acquaintance here."

"And my mother, of course," he added.

"Oh, yes . . . of course." Her response came out quietly, and she looked away from him.

His mother's presence didn't seem to please her, he noted. He wondered why, but he was well aware that the duchess could be haughty. Perhaps she'd said something to offend Miss Irvine.

As they reached the drawing room and took seats opposite the older women, he reminded himself to try to take advantage of this chance to learn more about her character. He cleared his throat. "I shall have to introduce you to some of my friends—assuming any show up tonight. Some of my bachelor acquaintances are considered quite eligible, I believe."

She cocked an eyebrow. "Surely you aren't prone to matchmaking, your grace?"

He glanced down to flick an imaginary speck of lint from his shoulder. "I only hope to be helpful. Naturally, a young marriageable woman will want to meet marriageable men."

"Not in my case."

Surprised, he looked back up at her, but she had turned toward the pianoforte, where the first performer of the evening was seating herself.

"You're not seeking a husband?" he asked. Then a thought occurred to him that—oddly—made him frown. "Or is it that you're betrothed already?"

She shook her head and peered at him from the corner of her eye. "I don't intend to marry. I have other plans."

Before he could question her further—or, indeed, decide whether or not doing so would be rude—the music began and all talk hushed. As Lady Louisa labored at the keys of the pianoforte, Miss Irvine's statement nagged at him. It was strange for a young, attractive woman to forswear marriage, but, more to the point, if she didn't plan to marry, how did she intend to support herself?

Obviously she meant to leech off her rich aunt.

He stewed all through the song, barely conscious of the performance. When he noticed the audience around him clapping, he joined in to be polite.

His mother leaned toward him and whispered, "Quite an execution, eh? The gel is as talented as she is beautiful."

"Mmm," he acknowledged vaguely.

As a second young lady began to play, this one on the

harp, another event distracted him: the arrival of his presumed heir, Charles Leight. Per usual, the young fop wore pastel satins with a host of fobs pinned upon him.

Watching him acknowledge a dozen nods and smiles before taking a seat, Adrian frowned. At one time he had found Charles as charming as many others still appeared to, but the fellow had ended up disappointing him. A year ago, Adrian had invited his cousin to his country estate to teach him about managing the property that would likely one day be his. Unfortunately, Charles had been more interested in gambling and wenching at the local tavern. In two months, he'd scarcely listened to two days' worth of Adrian's tutelage.

His annoyed stare drew the lad's attention. Spotting him, Charles beamed and nodded.

Adrian gave a curt nod back and looked away, feigning interest in the performance. After a few moments of cringing over the young woman's missed notes, he was relieved when the song reached a conclusion.

When the smattering of applause faded, Lady Postlethwaite rose and announced a break for refreshments.

Within seconds, Charles was standing next to Adrian's chair, exclaiming over his luck in encountering his relatives.

"You must introduce me to your companion, Cousin," he said, after greeting everyone in the vicinity whom he already knew. He glanced at Miss Irvine and smiled. "I don't believe I've seen this lady in London before."

Adrian drew in a deep breath, annoyed that the milksop would likely proceed to fawn all over the American. He looked at her, wondering how she would respond. Would Charles's fair good looks and vibrant youth reverse her disinterest in bachelors? "Miss Irvine, may I present my cousin, Mr. Charles Leight? Charles, Miss Maeve Irvine of Boston, Massachusetts."

The two exchanged pleasantries, speaking easily with one another. Apparently, Miss Irvine could banter with *any* fellow she'd just met. After a moment, Charles sat down beside her.

Adrian crossed his arms over his chest.

"Lady Louisa is such a fine player," his cousin said. "Of course, Miss Higgins offered us a commendable performance, as well. Do you play a musical instrument, Miss Irvine?"

She shook her head. "My only talent is for painting, I'm afraid."

"You are a painter?" Charles nudged his chair closer to her. "Do you render portraits?"

"I do."

Lady Blaine leaned toward them. "My niece is quite accomplished, Mr. Leight. She was among the first women admitted to the Boston Academy of Fine Arts."

"Indeed?" Charles rubbed his chin. "How interesting."

Adrian nearly rolled his eyes, certain that his cousin's fascination was no more than an attempt to flatter Miss Irvine. Luckily, he was saved from listening to further nonsense when the musical performances resumed.

Throughout the next two songs, however, Charles continually found reasons to bend close to Miss Irvine and whisper comments only she could hear. She didn't answer him, evidently too well-bred to talk over the music, but her smiles voiced her amusement. Adrian couldn't help but feel a twinge of jealousy.

More important, with the way Charles was dominating her attention, he couldn't take advantage of the opportunity to pump her for information!

As the minutes ticked by, his mood only darkened.

Likely he wouldn't be able to squeeze in another two words to Miss Irvine. A stick-in-the-mud like he could hardly compete with a young dasher like Charles.

His gut burning with frustration, he looked away and vowed to avoid watching the pair.

Maeve sensed a stare upon her and glanced over to see the Duke of Ashton quickly look away. He focused on the woman playing pianoforte, his arms crossed over his chest. His obviously sour mood disappointed her. She had been looking forward to more bantering with him tonight, she realized.

Mr. Leight leaned toward her again and whispered, "You say you're seeking commissions to paint?"

She nodded, uncomfortable with carrying on a conversation while others were trying to listen to the music.

The young man studied her closely. "I've never met a formally trained artist before. I'd very much like to view your work."

"My aunt has several of my paintings on display in her house."

"Lady Blaine does?" He glanced toward the countess and nodded to himself. "I'll ask her ladyship if I can call there—assuming you don't mind."

She was surprised, but she saw no harm in agreeing. Apart from a slight lack of manners, the man seemed respectable. After all, he was cousin to the duke. Besides, he seemed genuinely interested in her art rather than in her person. She nodded to him. "I'd be honored."

Another song ended, and the audience clapped politely.

Mr. Leight rose and moved closer to her aunt. After a few remarks on the performance, he asked her, "May I call on you and Miss Irvine some time soon, my lady?"

She gave him a radiant smile. "Of course you may."

"Excellent. Thank you." He turned to say a few words to the duchess, then excused himself to mingle with other acquaintances.

As he walked away, Maeve noticed the duke watching him, his expression practically a scowl. Even meeting his cousin hadn't cheered him tonight. She wondered what was bothering him. Surely it wasn't merely his reputed dislike of socializing.

She moved her chair closer to his. "I can't help but notice that you're not enjoying yourself. I hope you didn't come here on my account."

His gaze shot to meet hers, his look startled. "What do you mean?"

"I suspect my aunt pressed you to attend." Now that she considered it, that was probably why he'd offered to introduce her to his friends. "Was it she who asked you to throw eligible bachelors in my path?"

"Oh—er, no." He still appeared distracted, clearly bothered by something. "As I told you, that was my own idea—misguided, evidently. I must say I don't believe I've ever before met a young woman who had forsworn marriage."

She looked down into her lap. The subject still pained her, despite the passage of time. Would her wounds ever completely heal? "My painting is my highest priority. I don't believe a husband would quite understand that."

"A serious pursuit in life seems beneficial to me, though I suppose some men might object. But . . . well, frankly, do you have the means to live independently?"

Unwilling to lie outright, she chose evasion. Forcing herself to meet his eye, she said, "My painting will eventually earn me something, and I don't require much. I'm fortunate in that Aunt Eleanor has taken me in."

He frowned, then opened his mouth as if about to ask

her more—but at that moment his mother stepped up, arm in arm with their hosts' daughter.

"Adrian, I was just telling Lady Louisa how eager you were to attend tonight." The duchess tugged on the girl to draw her closer and said to her, "My son doesn't often attend musical evenings, my dear, only when he's convinced the performances will be exceptional."

The duke rose and bowed to the musician, a petite debutante with even features, a fresh complexion, and a head full of glossy black curls. "Your performance lived up to all expectations."

A hint of a blush tinted her cheeks attractively. She smiled and batted her sooty lashes. "Thank you, your grace."

Maeve frowned to herself, inexplicably annoyed. She supposed she had lost her patience for simpering coquettes when she'd renounced flirtation herself.

"Miss Irvine, would you like to play a song or two for us this evening?" Lady Louisa asked her, proving she had good breeding, if not wisdom about men.

Maeve smiled and thanked her but declined with certainty.

The group chatted a few moments longer. Then Lady Louisa moved on. The duchess returned to her seat, but leaned over to make a remark to her son, too quiet for Maeve to hear. Maeve noticed that the duke had already taken up his scowl again. Luckily, another group of performances was beginning, rescuing her from having to try to cheer him.

The evening didn't improve as it wore on. Though the duke seemed to hover near her during the breaks in music, he had little to say. Instead of bantering with her as he had at the docks and earlier that day, he posed only a few odd questions about her life in America. She had to answer vaguely so as not to reveal her wealth, and the conversation lagged.

When she and her aunt were riding home from the gathering, she remarked on the duke's ill mood.

The older woman twisted her mouth and sighed. "Yes, I noticed, too—and he was in such good spirits this morning. I'd hoped he'd be his old self tonight, but he was in one of his dark moods. Ever since he returned from the Peninsula, he's been a little peculiar."

Maeve pulled her shawl around her more tightly to fend off the chill of the evening. "The duke fought against Napoleon?"

Her aunt nodded. "And very bravely, bringing home a number of honors. Sometimes I think he sacrificed more for our country than he should have. He may have helped to win a few battles, but he lost something inside—something valuable."

"What did he lose?"

"I suppose you'd call it joie de vivre. He used to be so carefree. Even after his father died and Adrian had to take on ducal responsibilities at a young age, he managed to retain a light heart." Her aunt looked out the carriage window. "But not after the war."

Recalling his playful manner at the docks, Maeve wondered if Aunt Eleanor were painting her son-in-law rather darker than he was in reality. "Surely he has his moments of cheer."

"Yes . . . I don't mean to imply he *never* smiles or laughs. Indeed, little Eliza is clearly a joy to him. He's simply not the same as he once was." Without turning around, she shrugged. "Jane hopes he'll find happiness in remarrying."

Her tone didn't sound optimistic, Maeve noted. "Do you doubt it?"

She hesitated. "I'm not sure. Frankly, being with Belinda didn't seem to help him fight whatever demons he's facing—but perhaps she didn't offer him enough compassion." She met Maeve's gaze briefly, then looked away again. "I fear that as an only child, my daughter never quite learned to place others before herself. My dear Arthur spoiled her to the quick . . . and I confess I did almost as badly."

Maeve smiled softly. "If my cousin was anything like her mother, I'm sure she did all she could for those she loved."

"I'm afraid that as a wife she may have been more demanding than giving. Belinda had a head full of romantic notions and was accustomed to a good deal of attention. Adrian could not always appease her the way her father and I had."

"Well, a husband ought to give a wife all the attention she needs," Maeve said. After being abandoned by Thomas, she had no tolerance for men whose devotion waned at the first test. She wondered if the duke were a bit cold, as Englishmen were sometimes said to be.

"When a man is in the king's service, he doesn't have much time for anything else," her aunt said. "Of course, Belinda was angry that Adrian went to war at all, especially the second time, when she was *enceinte.*"

Maeve stiffened. "He went to war while she was expecting?"

Aunt Eleanor said nothing, only lifted her hands, palms up.

"But surely a man as powerful as the Duke of Ashton could have sold his commission and stayed home for the birth of his child. A man should remember that love always comes first."

Her aunt smiled sadly and shook her head. "I see that you have a few youthful, romantic notions of your own."

"I'm not in the least romantic. Over the past year I've

put all of those schoolgirlish ideas behind me. I simply don't like to see a man forget a woman."

"Adrian never forgot Belinda. Only look at what a social recluse he's become since her death."

Maeve considered the point. The sympathy she had read in the duke's face at the mention of her father's death proved that he knew the depths of grief. She remained unconvinced, however, that he understood the meaning of true love.

Or if any man did, for that matter.

Sighing, she reached out to take her aunt's hand. "Losing her must have been awful for both of you. I'm so sorry."

"Thank you, dear, but I admire the philosophy you prescribed when you first arrived. I, too, have had it with melancholy. Thank heavens I have little Eliza to cheer me." She squeezed Maeve's hand. "And now I have my lovely niece here as well. I almost hope you do as you say and don't get married—not too soon, anyway. I want to keep you to myself for a while."

Maeve let out a short, humorless laugh. "I'm confident you'll get your wish."

A lump formed in her throat, however. What a joy it would be to have a little daughter like Eliza. She turned toward the window, blinking against tears. How could the duke have been so apathetic about the birth of his first child? Men were like a different species altogether.

She tried to swallow her emotions. Her resolve against marriage was firmer than ever.

Why, then, did her decision seem to make her less happy than ever? Would she never quite come to accept her lot in life?

# Five

On the morning following the musicale, Maeve sat in the parlor reading while her aunt netted. The sound of a carriage slowing outside on the street made them look up.

"I wonder who that could be," Aunt Eleanor said, stretching her neck to try to see the street from her chair. "Jane will be too busy preparing for her dinner party tonight to stop by today."

*Busy enough to keep her son at home, too?* Maeve wondered, but she didn't ask because she didn't want to appear more interested in the duke than she was. In fact, she didn't want to appear as interested *as* she was. Even after learning of his neglect of Belinda, she couldn't quite shake off her fascination with him. The same man who had ignored his pregnant wife had reacted to her death by practically becoming a social recluse. Was he coldhearted or was he not?

The sound of muffled men's voices drifted into the room from the hall. Webster open the doors, but it was not the duke he ushered in.

"Mr. Charles Leight," the butler announced.

With a faint feeling of disappointment, Maeve rose to greet the man. As she smiled and gave him her hand, she admonished herself inwardly. She would see the duke at his mother's that evening. Surely one encounter with him a day would be enough to satisfy her curiosity about him.

After everyone had exchanged greetings, the countess offered their guest a chair.

"Thank you, my lady." He bowed and seated himself. "And thank you for receiving me."

"Not at all." The countess smiled and set down her netting needles. " 'Tis about time you've paid me a call at home. You are family, after all."

He returned a warm grin. "True. I've been remiss—but I may well be stopping here frequently in the near future."

"Is that so?" The countess lifted an eyebrow and glanced at Maeve before looking back to him.

He, too, glanced at Maeve, then cast his gaze downward briefly, more of a token show of shyness than a convincing gesture. "That depends on Miss Irvine."

Maeve swallowed. Did he want to court her after all? *Good Lord.* She hoped her aunt wouldn't encourage him unduly.

Mr. Leight met her gaze and grinned again. "I came to learn more about your painting. Was that portrait in the hallway one of yours, by any chance?"

She nodded, confused. Was he simply an art lover? "A portrait of my father that I brought with me."

"Marvelous. The detail is excellent. I'm no artist myself, but I know good brushwork when I see it."

"Thank you." She tilted her head to one side. "Are you a collector, then?"

"Oh, no." He pushed back his pale hair, then stood. For a instant, he looked genuinely unsure of himself. "Forgive me, but before I say more, I'm going to have to ask for the discretion of both of you ladies. I'd like to commission a painting, but it's to be a surprise. You would have to keep absolutely silent about it. Would you be comfortable with that?"

Maeve relaxed somewhat, relieved to learn he had an

impersonal reason for coming. She scooted forward in her chair. "The prospect sounds intriguing. I don't mind being temporarily sworn to secrecy. Aunt Eleanor, would you be willing to keep mum on Mr. Leight's behalf?"

The older woman hesitated. "I suppose there would no harm in it, as long as the secret involves nothing dishonorable. Do you mean to present the painting as a gift, Mr. Leight?"

He nodded, his grin spreading. " 'Tis for my fiancée—but you must keep mum about the betrothal, too. We aren't making an announcement for several weeks."

Maeve smiled, too. He definitely didn't want to court her.

A frown crinkled her aunt's brow, however. "I'm afraid I must ask if you have the approval of the young lady's parents."

"Yes, ma'am." Mr. Leight remained standing, but leaned on the back of his chair and crossed one leg over the other.

"Then why the secrecy?"

Again, he looked downward, but his irrepressible grin prevented his looking shy. "My fiancée is a very romantic girl, my lady. She's always had a desire to announce her betrothal at her own come-out ball."

Maeve giggled. "Goodness, that will cause a stir. 'Tis indeed romantic, and I admire your wish to indulge the woman you love. Will the portrait be a likeness of you?"

He nodded. "I fear I may look a bit conceited in the eyes of onlookers, but I believe *she* will be pleased."

"No doubt." Maeve sat back in her chair. "Well, I will be honored to help you."

"One moment, please." The countess held up a hand. "I have a few more questions. Mr. Leight, I still must ask what *your* family thinks of the girl. Is your mother aware of your intentions?"

He lifted his chin. "She has a good idea of them—and, yes, she is quite fond of my choice. But surely, my lady, you don't expect a grown man to seek the approval of his mother before selecting a wife?"

"Most people want their parents' blessing."

"My mother has always given me her blessing when she knows I have my mind set on something. Frankly, she'll be glad to see me settled—and I daresay my extended family will, too."

"Hmm." She bit her thumbnail in thought. "I don't suppose you'll tell *us* the girl's identity."

"Not yet, but I *will* when Miss Irvine has finished the painting. I'd like both of you there when I present it. Don't worry. I'm confident you would have attended my fiancée's ball anyway. I'm sure you've socialized with her family before."

Finally, Aunt Eleanor nodded and picked up her netting again. "Very well. I apologize for my interrogation, but secrets always make me nervous."

"Perfectly understandable. I appreciate your effort to protect me, unfounded as your concern was." He reseated himself and turned to face Maeve. "Now let's discuss a fee for your work. Tell me what is fair, and I'm certain I can agree."

Maeve took a moment to think. She posed several questions about the size of the work and what sort of setting he envisioned for the backdrop. After estimated what materials and time she would need for the painting, she quoted him a modest fee. He accepted readily, and they made plans for him to return in two days for his first sitting. Then he stood to leave, and Maeve rose in turn.

He shook her hand with vigor. "I can't wait to get started."

"I look forward to it, too," she said. The romance of the plan appealed to her. His fiancée was a lucky woman.

The countess looked up from her work. "Thank you again for calling, Mr. Leight. Will we see you at Jane's dinner party this evening?"

"Oh, yes, I nearly forgot about that." He put a hand up to his mouth. "Dear me. You must promise you won't mention any of this to my aunt and cousin. Neither of them are much for romance. I'd prefer to surprise them along with the rest of the *ton*. They should be present at my fiancée's ball, too. I must say I like the idea of setting the *ton* on its ear. It will be such good fun."

Aunt Eleanor shook her head, but a twinkle in her eye betrayed her amusement. "I hope all goes as you plan."

"Thank you, my lady." He walked to the door and bid them farewell until that evening.

When he'd gone, Maeve reseated herself and grinned at her aunt. "He is an energetic fellow, isn't he?"

She nodded. "I only hope this gel is as good for him as he believes. Frankly, Jane has confided in me that she feels Charles is a little wild. It seems Adrian was disappointed a few years back when he attempted to instruct the boy in estate matters. Charles is Adrian's presumed heir, you know."

Maeve raised her brows. "No, I didn't. Won't Eliza inherit his wealth, then?"

"Not the bulk of it, but she is well set, I assure you. Adrian will provide her with a substantial dowry, and when I die she'll inherit the majority of my estate."

"Well, she's not likely to go hungry then, is she?" Somehow it still seemed a shame that the duke's prestigious title wouldn't pass to a descendant of his—unless he remarried and had a son, of course. She rubbed her chin in thought. "Do you think the duke will remarry?"

Her aunt shrugged, but a hint of a smile tugged at her

lips. "I had believed he'd sworn it off, but now I'm not certain. Though he may have been moody last night, he was quite attentive to you. He scarcely left your side."

Maeve reflected on the evening and was surprised to realize it was true. "But he didn't act particularly taken with me. Oddly, he seemed curious about my financial state. Maybe he wants to enlist me, as a poor relation, to help care for Eliza."

"Perhaps we should reveal the true state of your finances and see if enlists you as her stepmother."

She stiffened. "If he needs to know I have money in order to want to marry me, I don't want him anyway."

Her aunt smiled softly and looked down at her work. "I doubt your money would be the deciding factor. Let's see how he behaves toward you tonight."

Maeve frowned, suspecting she had shown more emotion than she should have. She considering protesting her indifference further but decided that changing the subject might prove wiser. "Will you keep your promise to Mr. Leight and not tell the duchess about his plans?"

Aunt Eleanor twisted her mouth but nodded. "To be candid, I have no desire to tell Jane about the portrait. She's not likely to approve of your taking money for your services."

Maeve had to stop herself from blurting out that she didn't care what the duchess thought. Unfortunately, her aunt *did* care. A sort of compromise occurred to her. "Perhaps I could give the portrait to Mr. Leight and his fiancée as a betrothal gift. As you pointed out, he is family."

Her aunt's gaze shot to meet hers. "Would you be willing to do that?"

She laughed. "Certainly. I hardly need the money. But let's not say anything about it to Mr. Leight until the painting's done. I'll simply tell him I won't accept any money from him before then."

"Very well." Aunt Eleanor's shoulders relaxed visibly. "Meanwhile I intend to deduce who this girl is who has him entranced. There are only so many debutantes and come-out balls this Season. If she's respectable, his secret is safe with me. If not, I'll have to rethink matters."

Maeve just shook her head to herself. Sometimes her aunt could be rather unromantic.

As Adrian turned into Grosvenor Square, he saw a swarm of liveried carriages outside of his town house. Only then did he remember his mother's dinner party.

When she had told him about it the week before, he'd warned her he had a meeting with his estate manager and might be late. She had read his mind and denied arranging the party to parade some worthy debutante in front of him, but now he recognized the Postlethwaites' crest on one of the equipages. Lady Louisa would be among the guests.

Slowing the horses in front of the house, he frowned. There was Charles's phaeton, another guest he'd rather avoid. A groom was driving Lady Blaine's coach around back toward the stables, providing a more welcome sight. Adrian wondered if he'd have much luck speaking to Miss Irvine tonight. He still wasn't sure exactly what questions to ask her. His numerous financial inquiries were beginning to sound impertinent. Perhaps he needed to escort her alone on some sort of outing and try to get to know her. But where could they go? Maybe a museum would prompt her to open up and reveal who she really was.

He stopped the carriage and jumped down from the box, passing the reins to his tiger. A quick check of his pocket watch revealed he had just enough time to change before the meal was served. To avoid being waylaid, he entered a side door and stole upstairs.

When he walked into the dining room some ten minutes later, the guests were just taking their seats.

"Adrian, I am so pleased you could make it." His mother sat at the foot of the table, her face radiant. She didn't normally relish entertaining, so he feared she had high hopes for her latest protégée.

He nodded to her and murmured an apology to the guests in general. Glancing over the party, he noted it was small enough that a single conversation might be followed by all. As he scanned the group, Miss Irvine's gaze caught his. Dressed in a simple dark blue dress, she looked lovely and elegant, but somewhat somber compared to the others. She nodded to him without smiling, then turned to her dinner partner: Charles.

Trying not to scowl, Adrian took his place at the head of the table. Lady Louisa and her mother sat on either side of him. He gave each a wavering smile and reached for the glass of champagne at his setting.

*I should have had a brandy in my chamber before coming down,* he thought.

"Adrian, I'd like to reintroduce you to several of our guests." His mother's voice commanded attention, even from the other end of the table. "To my left is Lord Paterson, Lady Blaine's neighbor on South Audley Street. To my right is his good friend, Colonel Westfall."

"Ah, yes." Adrian lifted his glass in greeting. "We met in the park a few weeks ago. A pleasure to see you both again."

The men expressed their gratitude for the dinner invitation.

As two footmen entered bearing trays of soup, Adrian

asked, "Colonel, are you the Westfall who fought with the ninth regiment in the Peninsula?"

"One and the same." The corners of the man's eyes crinkled. "And, of course, I'm aware that you are the Ashton who distinguished himself leading the fourteenth. Your reputation for bravery precedes you."

Adrian looked into his drink. "Bravery, in my case at least, is nothing more than being at the right place at the wrong time. I did no more than most would have done had they been called upon."

"You are too modest. Very few would have come back to the Peninsula for a second round after being sent home with typhus."

He shrugged, always uncomfortable thinking back on that time of his life. The truth was that he didn't even remember many events from that era—only pain. "The fever had long subsided before I went back. Anyone in my situation would have done the same."

"Do you think so?" a feminine voice asked. Miss Irvine focused her deep blue eyes upon him with an unusual intensity. "Your 'situation' encompassed a large estate, a young wife, and no heir. I don't believe *I* should have gone back under the circumstances."

Naturally, she had no concept of the rest of his circumstances at the time. Not bravery but disillusion with Belinda had spurred him to return to war, but of course he could not say so. "I was needed. It is that simple."

She lifted her chin as if to challenge him. "How can you possibly call it simple?"

He frowned. How unfortunate that she should choose to probe the one topic he least wished to discuss. And why did she look so serious about it?

"Believe me, Maeve," Lady Blaine said, saving him from having to answer, "at the time, Jane, Belinda, and I all felt as you do, and we told Adrian as much. He would not hear us. I suppose that is why men go to war and women do not. But, please, let us speak of something more pleasant."

She turned to the two older men. "Do you gentlemen intend to attend Alexandra Trent's come-out ball on Thursday? Lady Olivia has invited enough of the *ton* to ensure it will be the first big crush of the Season."

"I wouldn't miss it for the world." Lord Paterson pushed his empty soup bowl away from him. "Having been away from town for several years, I've dearly missed grand balls. I am exceedingly fond of dancing."

"Are you?" The duchess beamed. Looking to the gentleman opposite him, she asked, "And you, Colonel Westfall, will we find you on the dance floor as well?"

The man chuckled, dabbing at his snowy moustache with a napkin. "If so, I fear you may regret being subjected to my lack of grace. There was a time when I danced a tolerable reel or two, but I confess I haven't even tried in years."

"Never fear, Colonel, dancing is among those skills that never abandon one." The duchess leaned closer to him, her eyelashes fluttering. "Pray indulge us on Thursday."

Adrian stopped with his spoon in midair. Surely his mother wasn't flirting . . . was she?

"I shall certainly do so if I can prevail upon you to join me for a set, your grace," Westfall said, smiling. "And I even promise to practice between now and then."

She cast her gaze demurely downward. "I shall look forward to the honor."

Adrian almost choked on his soup. He had never before witnessed such coquettish behavior in his mother and found the experience rather embarrassing. Gulping down the broth, he asked, "Miss Irvine, have you had much opportunity to explore London? The city boasts quite a few historical attractions, if your interests lies in that direction."

She gave him a smile that didn't reach her eyes. "I have a great interest in London's history, but, no I haven't yet seen much. I should love to visit the Tower of London and, most particularly, some of the museums, since art is my first love."

"I'm afraid I've kept Maeve too busy shopping since she arrived," Lady Blaine said, her features twisting with regret. She looked to her niece. "I shall accompany you sightseeing soon, love. I promise."

Miss Irvine shook her head. "No, Aunt Eleanor, I know you've already seen every attraction in town. I'll take my maid out with me when I find the time."

"I can show you about," Charles said. "In fact, if you're free tomorrow afternoon, I'll take you to the Tower then."

Something knotted in Adrian's stomach.

Miss Irvine looked at his cousin. "I need to shop for a few art supplies tomorrow. I'm eager to start working on my next painting."

He grinned. "No trouble. We'll pick them up on our way back from the Tower."

She nodded. "Excellent. Thank you, Mr. Leight."

Adrian let out an exasperated sigh. If he ever wanted a real chance to acquaint himself with Miss Irvine, it appeared he would have to escort her somewhere himself. Thinking out loud, he said, "Perhaps *I* can take you to a museum later in the week, Miss Irvine."

Her gaze shot to meet his—along with several other pairs of widened eyes.

"Are you not busy with estate accounts this week?" his mother asked him, her expression taut with annoyance. No doubt she felt Lady Louisa would be discouraged by his attention to another woman.

"I cannot keep my nose buried in ledgers twenty-four hours a day," he said firmly. "A visit to a museum would provide the perfect break for me."

She frowned but protested no more.

"What a kind offer, your grace," Miss Irvine said, her tone polite rather than excited. "If your schedule does indeed allow it, please let me know what day would be best for you."

He nodded, slightly disconcerted to have drawn so much notice to himself and his interest in her. "I'll check back with you in a few days."

For the rest of the meal, he kept fairly quiet. Out of courtesy, he asked the Postlethwaites a few questions, but he made sure not to distinguish Lady Louisa more than any other guest. Twice out of the corner of his eye he noticed Charles speaking sotto voce to Miss Irvine. On both occasions, she responded with a crooked grin full of mischief. When Lady Blaine mentioned that Charles had called on them that morning, Adrian felt inordinately annoyed—and he wasn't quite sure why.

He supposed Charles annoyed him in general.

After dinner, the ladies retired to the drawing room, and the men stayed behind for a glass of port. When Adrian had a chance, he pulled Charles aside to ask what his interest in Miss Irvine was. The lad claimed he'd only stopped by to view her art, adding that he'd been very impressed.

Adrian frowned. "Did she show you her sketchbook?"

"No, only a few paintings on display at the house. Why do you ask?"

"Just wondered." He turned away, feeling his first trace of satisfaction all evening. The feeling forced him to acknowledge that he was jealous of his cousin's rapport with Miss Irvine. Foolish. The woman had declared that she didn't want to marry, anyway. If it was true,

Charles was no more likely to change her mind than he himself.

Not that he was thinking of marrying her. What an absurd thought.

When the men rejoined the women, he quickly scanned the drawing room, but Miss Irvine wasn't present. Hoping she would return quickly, he avoided choosing a seat. After ten minutes of standing about, he grew impatient to know her whereabouts. Knowing that his mother wouldn't like him to inquire about her aloud, he moved next to Lady Blaine and asked softly, "Your niece is not ill, is she?"

She looked up at him with a mysterious smile and shook her head. "Maeve has gone to look in on Eliza."

The information took him aback. Miss Irvine had shown interest in the baby before, too, yet apparently she didn't want children of her own. *Curious.*

He spent another five minutes milling about, trying not to look distracted. Then he told the guests closest to him that he needed to check with the grooms about an ailing horse. He headed toward the kitchen, but instead of exiting the house, he took the service stairs and went to the nursery.

At the doorway, he stopped. Miss Irvine was sitting on the floor of the room, her back toward him. She lifted Eliza high and the baby laughed.

"Birdie!" Eliza exclaimed.

Miss Irvine giggled and hugged her. "You look like your papa when you smile—only you do it much more often than he."

She lifted the child in the air again, and Eliza spotted him over her head.

"Papa!" the baby greeted him.

"You love your papa, do you?" Miss Irvine asked. "Does he often play with you, I wonder?"

Adrian stepped into the room and cleared his throat. "Whenever I have a moment."

Miss Irvine started, then blushed.

The baby laughed and stretched her arms out to him.

He reached for Eliza and took her so the grown woman could scramble to her feet.

"You startled me," she said, putting one hand up to cover her heaving bosom.

Adrian fought to keep his attention on her face but allowed a grin to creep to his lips. "Sorry—but you shouldn't be pumping my daughter for information about me."

She cast her gaze downward but allowed herself a shy smile. "Perhaps not, but you'll be pleased to know that she has only good things to say about you."

"Well, what a relief. Thank you, Eliza." He kissed the baby's forehead and noted that her eyes were beginning to close. He walked her over to the crib and laid her down. "It's bedtime for you, young lady."

While he tucked the child in, Miss Irvine moved over to stand beside him at the crib.

"Eliza seems remarkably amenable to going to bed," she whispered. "Many toddlers put up some resistance, from what I understand."

He smiled as the baby tried—and failed—to keep her eyes open. "My daughter has always been a remarkably good girl."

"She must get her good behavior from you. My aunt maintains that Belinda was a bit willful."

The smile slid from his face.

Miss Irvine put a hand up to her mouth. "I'm sorry. That didn't come out in the affectionate way I meant it. Please know that I didn't intend to insult your wife's memory."

A snort escaped him. "No, you're quite right. Belinda was willful."

An awkward silence ensued while he stared at the baby, unwilling to meet Miss Irvine's gaze. He didn't want her to believe she'd offended him, but he couldn't think of a way to lighten the mood. If he'd gone on to tell an amusing anecdote about Belinda's quirky willfulness, that would have done the trick, but only one story about his former wife came to mind . . . and it didn't amuse him in the least.

"I think she's asleep." Miss Irvine touched his hand briefly, a gesture of compassion that surprised him. When his gaze shot to hers, she smiled faintly and motioned with her head for them to leave the nursery.

Without thought, he followed her into the hallway, leaving the door ajar behind them.

Miss Irvine walked to a crescent-shaped table near the top of the main staircase. The table served as a catchall for nonurgent posted items and calling cards. From the cluttered surface, she picked up a playbill and grinned. "*Troilus and Cressida.* I just read this while aboard ship."

Her enthusiasm surprised him, for he had seen the play a fortnight before and had not been impressed. "Yes, Mother persuaded me to escort her to the production at Covent Garden when we first arrived in town."

"Oh! I'm sorry I missed it."

"I cannot say I cared much for it." In fact, the play had touched upon a nerve. He felt his lip twitch at the memory.

Miss Irvine stared at him with wide eyes. "Why ever not?"

"Cressida starts out as such a promising lover for Troilus, seemingly very attached to him. Then, for no apparent reason, she ends up in the arms of another man." His voice cracked, and he paused to clear his throat, taking a step away from her. He pretended to straighten a portrait on the wall beside him. "Of course, I knew she would, as I'd read Homer's version of the story in school, but I still found myself asking *why.* Why does she do it?"

"She does it because he finds her so easily dispensable." The conviction in her voice startled him.

He shot a look at her, only to be more astonished by the sparks he saw in her eyes. All signs of pleasure had drained from her face.

"What do you mean? He obviously loves her."

She looked heavenward, then back at him. "Cressida has given herself to Troilus body and soul, yet he surrenders her to the Greeks without a word of objection. You call that love?"

He studied her face, trying to understand why she appeared angry. "You feel that Troilus should have opposed exchanging her for the prisoners? Miss Irvine, in a war, a soldier is expected to act for the good of the whole, not to forward his personal interests."

"I might have known *you* would say that." She crossed her arms over her chest. "The entire Trojan War is fought because Troilus's brother refuses to return *his* lover to the Greeks. For Helen, the Trojans will expend ships, blood, lives . . . but Cressida? She can be traded for a prisoner or two."

He frowned. "The differing views of two men about war's due hardly justify a woman's infidelity."

"Troilus let his duty to war interfere with his duty to love. But I cannot expect *you* to condemn him for that, can I?"

Recalling her earlier criticism of his return to war, he began to see that she wasn't merely discussing Troilus. What skewed version of his own story had she heard?

His eyes narrowed. “Miss Irvine, were you perhaps in correspondence with my wife while I was away at war?”

“I need not have corresponded with Belinda to understand what she must have felt.” She lifted her chin. “Just as I understand Cressida’s salving her self-esteem in the arms of Diomedes.”

His jaw dropped. She actually condoned infidelity! The chit was cut from the same wanton cloth as her late cousin.

The heat of suppressed rage rose under his collar. It took all of his will not to tell her so—to blurt out the true reason he’d deserted his wife. Jaw clenched, he hissed, “I’m afraid we shall never see eye to eye on this point. I think we had best get back to the others.”

“On that, I can agree.” Turning her back to him, she fled down the stairs.

Adrian remained still for several more minutes, appalled by the implications of their argument. At first he thought Miss Irvine must have corresponded with Belinda and knew the whole sordid story of his marriage. But he’d never heard Belinda mention her cousin and he recalled Lady Blaine expressing regret that the two had never made contact.

He took a deep breath. At least his shameful history remained a secret.

The tension he’d felt melted into disappointment. Maeve Irvine was *not* a respectable woman. She lacked the morality to see that infidelity was wrong. Pity the man who married her!

Instantly he remembered that she didn’t plan to marry, a concept he’d found strange from the start. He didn’t believe her excuse about her painting excluding marriage. Surely she could find a husband interested in art.

What was the real reason then? Didn’t she want to commit to one man? Did she intend to string along lover after lover, living on Lady Blaine's wealth? Perhaps she'd already had a dozen lovers in Boston before crossing the ocean to set herself up here as respectable. Perhaps she'd *had* to leave because no one there would receive her anymore.

He turned back toward the servants' stairs. The woman's deception alarmed him. How would he protect his mother-in-law from her? One thing was certain: He couldn't continue this haphazard "investigation" of her. He had to come up with some sort of plan.

Pausing for one last listen at the nursery door, he walked to the stairs. The time had come for serious reflection. A trip to the stables would help clear his mind, as well as make his answers more believable if he were asked about the horses.

In any case, he didn't want to go back to the drawing room. He no longer felt equal to socializing.

# Six

Maeve stepped back and compared the pencil sketch on her canvas to the subject, who sat across the room from her. Fortunately, Aunt Eleanor had kept her late husband's old art studio intact and didn't mind if Maeve put the room to use. With two floor-to-ceiling windows and an northern aspect, the room offered ideal lighting.

Tapping her pencil on her chin, she nodded to herself. "That should suffice for today, Mr. Leight. I've got all of the basic lines down."

He grinned and let his posture slump, shifting one foot from his stool to the floor. "May I have a peek?"

"Well, this is only the preliminary sketch, but certainly you may look, if you wish."

Springing up, he strode to her side of the easel and gawked at the canvas. "Why, it's marvelous! You flatter me. I must confess I'm pleased that you've omitted my freckles."

She put a hand to her mouth to hold back a giggle. "This isn't the final piece, Mr. Leight—but if you have freckles, they are certainly inconspicuous, so I shall leave them out of the painting, too."

Aunt Eleanor, acting as chaperon for the sitting, put down her needlework and rose from her armchair to join them. " 'Tis a good likeness. You've captured that carefree expression of Mr. Leight's. I look forward to seeing the final work."

"Yes, I can scarcely wait." Mr. Leight tore his gaze away from the canvas to look at Maeve. "If you'd like to start painting now, I can sit for another hour or so."

"No, no. I won't need you for the next step," she said quickly. Between the hours he'd visited today and their trip to the Tower the day before, she'd had enough of his company for the time being. He was a genial enough fellow, but he and she had no significant areas of common interest. "I'll do as much of the painting as I can without requiring you to pose. Then I'll bring you back to refine the details."

"I appreciate your consideration. I suppose I have tarried rather long today." He pulled a watch from his pocket and checked the face. "Oh, yes. 'Tis later than I thought. The fellows at my club will wondering where I am."

"Best run along then." She tossed her pencil and eraser into her equipment box. "Shall we make an engagement for you to come by, say, on Thursday morning?"

"Sounds perfect." He shook her hand. "I'll see you then, Miss Irvine."

He thanked her aunt and then Maeve again and finally made his way out of the house.

After they had seen him to the door, Aunt Eleanor turned to her and sighed. "Phew. I never realized what a talkative fellow Charles is. With him posing, you must have had a hard time concentrating on your work."

Maeve laughed. "A bit."

The older woman turned toward the drawing room. "Shall I ring for tea now?"

"Yes, please. I'll clean up in the studio and join you in a few minutes."

Maeve returned to the studio and packed up the rest of her pencils and a T square she'd been using. She stashed her canvas in a storage cupboard, as she often did with unfinished pieces.

As she stepped into the hall, a knock sounded at the front door. Webster appeared almost instantly and admitted the Duchess of Ashton. From several yards behind him, Maeve caught the woman's eye and smiled a greeting.

"The countess is the drawing room, your grace," the butler said. "I'll announce you immediately."

"Actually, Webster, I'd like to have a word with Eleanor's niece first." She looked over his shoulder at Maeve. "Miss Irvine, is there somewhere you and I can speak in private?"

Maeve blinked at her, unable to fathom what confidential business she and the duchess could have. Was she perhaps planning some sort of surprise for Aunt Eleanor? But the woman's upturned nose and haughty features hardly radiated the warmth of friendship. "Of course, your grace. Come into the library."

The duchess followed her into the nearby room and closed the door behind them. She turned to face Maeve and tossed her head. "Miss Irvine, I shan't waste your time or mine by being coy. I just met my nephew Charles outside, and he told me he spent the last two afternoons with you. What's more, his manner was rather . . . secretive. In short, I have the notion that he has set his sights on you as a marital prospect."

"Oh, no, your grace." Maeve cast her gaze downward, embarrassed by the false assumption, especially since she couldn't reveal the real reason for Mr. Leight's visit today. "I'm sure you are mistaken."

"I think not." The woman stepped closer and puffed up her chest. "I'm afraid I have to caution you that

Charles is not an eligible parti for you. Though he may tell you he is in line to inherit Adrian's title and fortune, my son is only ten years his senior and may easily outlive the boy."

Maeve shot her a look, her shyness instantly vaporized. The old witch was implying that she was after Mr. Leight for money. *How ironic.* She crossed her arms over her chest. "That doesn't signify to me, as I am not seeking a husband."

The duchess let out a snort. She walked up to a large bouquet on a pedestal and pulled out a carnation to hold to her nose. "If you feel you must persist with that story, go ahead, but in my experience, declared bachelors and spinsters alike renounce such vows the moment someone turns their heads."

Maeve sucked in her breath, fighting to remain polite for the sake of her aunt's friendship. Despite her efforts, she couldn't quite contain her vexation. "Frankly, your grace, I'm not certain my ambitions are your concern."

The woman looked up from her flower and frowned. "There is no need to snip at me, Miss Irvine. This warning is entirely for your own good."

Maeve nearly laughed. She had a good idea about the real purpose of the warning, and it was chiefly for the benefit of the duchess. The woman didn't want to see her precious nephew consorting with an American. No doubt Maeve's apparent lack of wealth made her even less acceptable. She raised her eyebrows. "If your concern is for me, then why have you excluded my aunt from this discussion?"

The woman hesitated, looking back down at the carnation. In a less certain tone, she said, "I wanted to speak openly without embarrassing you in front of Eleanor."

"I have no cause for embarrassment, your grace."

The duchess met her gaze again. "Then you truly would not consider an offer from Charles, if he were to make one?"

Maeve tapped her foot on the floor, annoyed that the woman would not abandon her impertinent line of discussion. "It would be pointless of me to say so, since you've already predicted I will change my mind if the event ever comes to pass."

"Then you admit you are not adverse to his attentions?"

"I'm not adverse to what attentions Mr. Leight has paid me. Since you will make what you will of that, I see no use in continuing this discussion. Now, if you will excuse me, your grace . . ." She turned and walked out of the room without giving her a chance to object.

As she stalked up the hallway, she heard the woman call after her, but she didn't turn back. Instead she dashed up the stairs. Running into Miss Grey in the hall, she asked the abigail to tell her aunt she couldn't join her for tea due to a sudden headache. The excuse was quickly becoming reality, as the tension in her seemed to be converging in her head.

She went to her chamber and lay down on her back, trying to calm herself. It was getting more and more difficult to hide her dislike for her aunt's friend. The woman made little effort to do the same for her! No wonder the duke had difficulty showing warmth, when he had a mother like that.

The thought of the duke made her frown. She didn't know whether or not to regret their confrontation at the duchess's dinner party. The memory of his pained reaction to her careless comment about Belinda's willfulness had haunted her ever since. She had seen signs of deep grief in him on more than one occasion.

Then again, he'd also made those dreadfully stoic comments about duty outweighing love.

She stared at the ceiling, her thoughts drifting back to her own past. When Thomas had deserted her for a woman with a larger fortune, he too had claimed he'd based his decision on duty—familial duty. He'd maintained that his family's fortunes were in such dire straits that he owed it to them to make the most advantageous marriage possible. *Her* fortune wasn't good enough when there was a slightly larger one to be had.

Were all men so quick to cast aside a woman?

She rolled over on her side and closed her eyes. What did it matter? She had given up all hope of marrying. Fortunately, she had the means to support herself, as well as a few loved ones to keep her company. There was even little Eliza to play with and dote upon.

Her lower lip quivered, and she bit it to stop the foolish display of emotion.

Though she would never have a child of her own, surely her beautiful little cousin would prove the next best thing.

Adrian had a productive meeting with his man of business and returned home earlier than he had in three days. When he entered the house, silence greeted him—an unusual treat. His day was going well.

As he stood in the front hall removing his driving gloves, the butler appeared. The servant informed him that the duchess had gone to visit Lady Blaine.

"Did she take my daughter with her?" Adrian asked.

"No, your grace. I believe Nurse just put Lady Elizabeth down for a nap."

Adrian dismissed the man and stole upstairs to peek in at his daughter. He found her sleeping peacefully and slipped out again unnoticed. Looking forward to a few hours to himself in the library, he started back downstairs.

When he'd descended halfway, however, the front door burst open and his mother stormed into the foyer. Her bonnet sat askew on her head, and her face looked flushed.

Glancing up, she spotted him and clenched her fists. "That gel! I can hardly credit her impertinence."

He frowned and rushed down the remaining steps. "What has happened to upset you, Mother? I thought you went to visit Lady Blaine."

"I did, but I barely spoke to Eleanor." She pulled off her bonnet and handed it to a footman entering the hall. Patting down her hair, she turned back to Adrian. "Join me in my sitting room, and I'll explain."

He followed her into a small room in the rear of the house. Once she'd closed the door, they sat down facing each other.

"It's that Maeve Irvine." She put her hand up to her brow. "She's got her cap set for Charles."

A sick lump knotted in his stomach, despite the fact that the news didn't surprise him. He had twice witnessed Charles focusing his charm on Miss Irvine and knew that the pair had made plans to visit the Tower of London together. Only her declarations that she wasn't seeking a husband had left any doubts of his cousin's success with her.

"Are you certain?" he croaked out.

His mother nodded and reached for a decanter of sherry that she kept on a side table. "She didn't deny it."

Adrian noticed that the duchess made it sound as if she had accused Miss Irvine of a crime. Wondering exactly what had happened, he cleared his throat. "How did such a topic even arise in conversation?"

She poured herself a cordial, then held the bottle over a second glass. "Would you like one?"

He shot a look heavenward, then nodded. "Please."

Accepting the drink from her, he downed a gulp of the syrupy stuff and coughed. "Well, Mother?"

She took a deep breath. "If you're thinking that I stuck my nose into the gel's business, I only did so in an attempt to help her. When I arrived at Eleanor's, I spotted Charles coming down the front steps outside. I remembered he had promised to take Miss Irvine out yesterday, and I asked if they'd been obliged to postpone the engagement until today. Well, he informed me that they had spent *both* afternoons together."

Adrian's lip curled in displeasure. Afraid he was showing more emotion than a casual observer should, he took another gulp of sherry to hide his expression. He didn't want his mother to discover he had a soft spot for Miss Irvine. The knowledge would only afford her another reason to lecture him.

She leaned back in her armchair. "Naturally, I was rather surprised. I noted to him that spending hour after hour with a woman for two days in a row indicated serious intentions toward her. He said in a sly tone that it could indicate any number of things. Imagine him teasing me! You are right about that boy lacking a proper sense of respect."

"Nevertheless, his flip comment may signify that he's only dallying with Miss Irvine." Adrian found himself hoping this were true. He didn't want to see her vows against marriage put to the test.

"I don't think so. The boy had a spark in his eye that looked like love to me." The duchess took a sip of her drink. "Naturally, as his aunt, I felt it my duty to warn him that Miss Irvine is no great match for him. The news didn't even seem to affect him. Perhaps he already knew about her financial circumstances. She's a bit too free with personal information for her own good. In any case, I suppose that as long as you have no son, Charles figures your fortune is as good as his."

A scowl twisted Adrian's features before he could school them into blandness. The thought of Charles' presumptions annoyed him, but only half as much his mother's taking advantage of the opportunity to remind him he ought to produce an heir.

He finished off the tiny drink and reached for the decanter to pour another. "This is all very interesting, Mother, but I thought it was Miss Irvine who upset you. You've only mentioned a conversation with Charles."

She held out her glass for him to top it off. "Well, after speaking to him with no success, I figured I'd try reasoning with her. She was in the hall when I entered the house, so I asked for a word in private. I tried to do the chit a favor and warn her Charles doesn't have the blunt she requires in a husband. Can you believe she ended up walking out of the room without waiting for my leave?"

He frowned as he poured her sherry. It was easy to imagine his mother failing to offer her advice in a diplomatic manner. "Is it possible that Miss Irvine got the impression you were accusing her of fortune hunting?"

"She *is* fortune hunting, Adrian. What other choice does a chit with no dowry have?"

*To flatter her way into a rich aunt's will,* he thought. Then another unpleasant idea occurred to him: If Miss Irvine *had* believed Charles was rich and interested in her, might she have seen him as a quicker way to financial security?

He set the decanter down. "How did she react when you told her about Charles's lack of fortune?"

"I told you she walked out on me—practically

slammed the door in my face. The news obviously didn't please her."

The behavior certainly sounded suspicious. He looked down into his glass.

His mother took a long sip of her drink and sighed. "When all is said, I suppose I may be overreacting. My confrontation with the gel was extremely vexing, but I have likely achieved my goal and turned her away from Charles."

Adrian considered her point. Part of him wished for her to be right—but if so, that only confirmed Miss Irvine was an unbridled fortune huntress. Whether he was only worried about Eliza's inheritance or he wanted to pursue Miss Irvine himself, that didn't offer him much comfort.

The duchess drained her glass and set it down. "I shall have to see how they behave toward each other at the Trents' ball on Thursday night."

"The Trents?" he asked, looking up at her. For years, he'd been avoiding balls, but he felt a need to see for himself what developed between his cousin and Miss Irvine. In fact, if their flirtation continued, he didn't want to sit back and watch. If Charles continued to dominate her attention, he'd be damned tempted to try to come between them.

*Come between them?* That was the key. A tingle of excitement shivered through him. Suppose he tried to test Miss Irvine's attraction to money by dangling his own wealth in front of her like a carrot?

"Yes, you know the Trents of Dorset," his mother said. "Eleanor told me she and Miss Irvine plan to attend their ball, and I'm sure Charles will go, too. I don't suppose you'd be willing to attend and give me your opinion of whether we have to worry about a disastrous mismatch in the family?"

A familiar twinkle lit up her eyes, and he realized her true reason for wanting him to attend: to press her latest protégée upon him, as usual. Looking away from her, he cleared his throat. "Seeing how upset you are about the situation, I suppose I will attend this once."

His comment precipitated a moment of stunned silence. Trying not to meet her gaze, he flicked an imaginary speck of lint from him sleeve.

"You will?" she sputtered at last.

He forced himself to look at her. "You did say you require my opinion?"

"Yes, yes, I did." Her voice took on a breathless quality. Still staring at him, she broke into a smile. "Thank you for this, Adrian. I know you're not overly fond of balls."

"My pleasure." Reluctant to endure further scrutiny from her, he stood to make his exit. "I must say, however, that I'd prefer you didn't press me to dance, or perform other social duties that I may seem to be avoiding. I will do as much I'm comfortable doing."

"That goes without saying." She gave a slight shake of the head, as if the idea of her nagging him were absurd. "I'll be happy merely to have you in attendance—and to hear your opinion on the matter we discussed, of course."

"Of course. We shall consider it an engagement then." He bowed to her and left the room.

On his way to the library, he wondered if he were mad, setting himself up to be hounded by his mother, but his heartbeat still raced with anticipation of the evening. He finally had a plan to test Miss Irvine's ethics. She had made clear the other day that she found him lacking in romantic dedication. He would make a point not to retract the statements he'd made about war coming before love, but he'd show more interest in her and drop hints about the wealth he had to offer. If she responded, then he'd know where her priorities lay.

*And if she doesn't respond?* he asked himself. Would he then open up to her and explain the real reason he'd placed the war before his marriage?

He drew in a long breath.

That was a matter he wasn't ready to speculate about. He would cross that bridge when he came to it . . . if indeed he ever did.

# Seven

"In the past quarter hour, we've moved only five houses closer," Aunt Eleanor said to Maeve as they waited in the press of carriages inching toward the Trent residence. "I suppose we should have made an earlier start."

"I hope I didn't hold up our departure by taking too long to dress." Maeve glanced at her reflection in the window of the carriage and tucked a straying lock of hair behind her ear. "The Trents must be a very prominent family among the *ton*. It looks as though all of fashionable London is here."

"Why, dear, you're not nervous, are you?"

"A little." Maeve turned around to face and her and forced a smile. "It is my first London ball. What if I make a terrible faux pas and embarrass you before the *ton*?"

"La, your manners are so artlessly sweet you could scarcely embarrass me if you tried." The duchess leaned out her open window to observe the queue. Pulling her head back inside, she said, "Actually, witnessing your first big appearance among the *ton* is about the only reason I'm excited about this ball."

"Why? I thought you enjoyed balls."

She shrugged and looked out the window again. "I do, for the most part."

Maeve frowned. Her aunt didn't seem her normal talkative self. She hoped the Duchess of Ashton hadn't mentioned the confrontation between the two of them. After the woman's visit, Aunt Eleanor had said only that her friend had been unusually reserved. Maeve hadn't had the heart to confess what had happened. "Is something troubling you—something to do with me?"

"Of course not! The truth is that I feel a bit neglected by Jane." The countess looked down to fiddle with one of the bows on her gown. "I never thought she'd be the sort to forsake a friendship as soon as a man entered her life, but I fear that is exactly what's happening."

"A man in her life?" Maeve thought back to the duchess's dinner party and her flirtation with one of the guests. "Do you mean Colonel Westfall?"

Her aunt nodded. "So you, too, noticed that she has a *tendre* for him."

"Well, she did seem interested in him that evening we all had dinner at Ashton House—but even if he returns her feelings, what makes you think she will forget your friendship?"

The countess sighed. "I've conjectured about her feelings for the colonel for some time, but her dinner party was the first occasion on which she's made them obvious. Ever since then, she's been behaving oddly toward me. I've never before felt so distant from her. She and I normally drive to balls together, for instance, but when I inquired about tonight, she told me she'd made plans to go with Adrian."

Maeve feared the duchess's aloof manner had more to do with her than her aunt. Her grace had likely not been pleased with her reaction to her offer of advice. She twisted her mouth. "Perhaps she's not yet ready to speak about her feelings for Colonel Westfall. She wouldn't want to set herself up for humiliation if it turns out he doesn't return her sentiments."

"But why not simply avoid discussing him rather than

avoid me altogether?" Her aunt shook her head. "I don't know. Maybe I am making too much of this. Before I make any further assumptions, I'll see how she behaves tonight."

"Good idea," Maeve said. She prayed the duchess would be in a good mood and end her aunt's fears.

After another half hour of creeping toward the house, the ladies alighted before the front doors. Making their way through the receiving line entailed another wait. By the time they entered the ballroom, Maeve had been introduced to several dozen people. The more she met, the more her confidence grew, for all were cordial, if not downright warm in their greetings. Not one person treated her with the haughtiness of the duchess.

As soon as they came upon the dance floor, a handsome but rather young gentleman who would someday be a baron asked Maeve to join him for a set. Next, a distinguished but decidedly middle-aged naval captain requested her hand. Then a marquis of an age more suitable asked her to stand up. Before she knew it, over an hour had flown by in a succession of pleasant but unremarkable partners.

During a perky country round, she spotted her aunt bolting by with Lord Paterson. He leaned toward his partner and made a comment, and both dancers laughed heartily.

When the set had ended and their partners had excused themselves, Maeve caught up with her aunt and gave her a broad grin. "I was pleased with my partner until I caught sight of yours and grew green with envy. Lord Paterson's rather handsome, is he not?"

"I suppose he is, in his way," she said, her voice breathless. She looked down at her gown and smoothed an invisible wrinkle. "I'm glad to see you enjoying yourself. To think you were afraid you'd have no acquaintances here! I noticed that your associate Charles Leight is present."

"Is he? I haven't seen him all evening."

"He arrived late, I believe." The countess glanced about the room. "Ah, there he is, talking to Alexandra Trent. Do you suppose she is the mystery woman to whom he is betrothed?"

Maeve spotted the pair, who appeared cheerful but unaffected by each other's presence. "I don't think so. His fiancée's ball must be later in the Season, don't you agree? He plans to present the portrait to her then."

"Oh, yes, of course. We'll have to keep an eye on how he treats the other debutantes present tonight and see if we can identify the right one."

"What about this one approaching him now?" Maeve asked as another woman adorned in diaphanous white joined the pair.

Her aunt followed the line of her gaze back across the room. "Miss Pamela Baylor? Hmm. Her approaching him and Miss Trent does seem somewhat forward, especially for a young woman just out. Yes, she scarcely greeted poor Miss Trent. The gel is definitely interested in Mr. Leight. Do you believe they appear to be in love?"

Maeve watched the couple laugh over something Mr. Leight said, their gazes fixed on one another. A twinge of longing surprised her. She looked away from the couple. "I really wouldn't know how to judge."

"'Tis rude of us to stare, anyway," her aunt said quickly. "Let's fetch ourselves some lemonade."

As they turned away, Maeve couldn't resist glancing back once more. The couple still gazed into each other's eyes, and she had to admit she envied them. How did one know if one had found true love?

Her prolonged look drew Mr. Leight's attention, even

from across the room. He looked over and nodded to her with a warm smile.

Miss Baylor noticed her fiancé's reaction and followed the line of his gaze to spot her, too. Embarrassed, Maeve gave them both a flickering smile and nod, then followed her aunt toward the refreshments.

In a curious chain reaction, she felt someone's eyes upon her and looked over to see the Duchess of Ashton watching her. When their gazes met, the woman pursed her lips. She must have observed the exchange between her and Mr. Leight and been vexed by their interaction.

Maeve met her stare evenly, determined not to cower. "Good evening, your grace."

"Hmm." The woman lifted her chin and looked away.

If her response wasn't the cut direct, it was the closest thing to it. Maeve's face heated with suppressed anger.

Aunt Eleanor glanced over her shoulder and saw her friend. She spun around with a broad smile. "Jane, you *are* here after all. I feared I wouldn't see you at all."

The duchess turned a stony countenance toward her. "Adrian and I have only just arrived."

Her aloof greeting made Maeve burn even hotter with anger. Just because the old harpy disapproved of *her* didn't mean she had to take it out on Aunt Eleanor! All this because Maeve hadn't accepted being judged a dreadful prospective marriage partner for the woman's silly nephew.

*Imagine how she would act if she knew the only man who really interests me is her precious son,* she thought, indignant. *Imagine if she knew about our little flirtation at the docks . . .*

Suddenly an imp stole up inside of her. She gave the duchess a saccharine smile. "And where is *Adrian,* your grace? I've been hoping for a dance with him all evening."

For an instant, an expression of shock usurped the woman's usual pomposity, but she soon turned her nose up again. "Adrian hasn't danced in years, so you shall have to make do without him. I'm sure you'll scarcely miss him with all your suitors to occupy you. However, to answer your question, he is sitting with Lady Louisa. They seem to be growing fond of each other lately."

The imp in Maeve shriveled, replaced by an envious shadow. Her feelings surprised her. Was she that vulnerable to the duke? She chided herself for goading his mother. Sinking to that level had gotten her only what she deserved.

Her aunt frowned. "Do you think so, Jane? They barely spoke to one another at dinner the other night, despite your seating them together."

"I know my own son, do I not?"

Poor Aunt Eleanor blinked at the curt answer. After a moment she recovered and said, "In any case, it would be wonderful if Maeve could persuade him to dance again. I asked Lady Jersey whether Maeve would be out of line to accept a waltz here, and she assured me it would be beyond reproach. Maeve isn't truly a debutante, you know."

"No, she isn't, but I don't see how that fact will win her favor with Adrian."

The countess's jaw dropped. "Jane, really!"

Maeve turned her face away, humiliated by the insult and sorry to be the cause of conflict for her aunt.

The duchess cleared her throat. "I apologize if that remark sounded unflattering, Miss Irvine. I meant only that you're no more likely to persuade my son to dance than numerous other women who have tried. By all means, do your best. No one would rather see Adrian dancing again more than I."

At that point, the next gentleman listed on Maeve's

dance card arrived to claim her hand, so she was spared further discussion of the topic. Taking the young man's arm, she nodded to the ladies and stepped back out on the floor.

During the set she alternatively steamed over the duchess's arrogance and wilted with her own insecurities. How stupid she had looked pretending that she thought she could entice the duke. She hadn't even been able to keep her own two-bit fiancé back home in Boston. Who would believe she could attract a wealthy and powerful man like Adrian?

*Adrian.* She had even called him by his given name to his mother's face. Her cheeks blazed with embarrassment.

After the set was over, she made an excuse to her partner and sought the less crowded perimeter of the room. A cool breeze blew in through an open outside door and brought relief to her still burning face. She glanced around and, not seeing her aunt to inform her of her intentions, slipped through the door to the terrace.

The night wasn't chilling, but brisk enough to invigorate her. She sucked in a deep breath, already soothed by solitude and the beauty of the evening. A striking full moon gleamed down from the clear, star-speckled sky. The ambience reminded her of the moonlight scene between Jessica and Lorenzo in *The Merchant of Venice.*

She stepped up to the wrought-iron rail at the edge of the terrace and continued to inhale the cool air of the night, along with the tranquillity it afforded. As her eyes adjusted to the light, she made out the trees, bushes, benches, and statues outlined in the moonlight.

" '*In such a night as this,*' " she recited softly to herself, " '*when the sweet wind did gently kiss the trees, and they did make no noise—in such a night, Troilus, methinks, mounted the Trojan walls and sighed his soul toward the Grecian tents where Cressid lay that night.' "*

Adrian wove his way through the throng, the lemonade he'd promised Lady Louisa splashing over the side of the glass onto his hand. Privately cursing his mother for stranding him with the debutante, he scoured his brain for an excuse to get away.

When he reached her, he handed her the drink and tried to smile. "I, er, believe I spotted an old schoolmate of mine while fetching your lemonade. If you'll pardon me, I'd like to try to catch up with him before he leaves."

"Oh, of course." A hint of pink tinged her cheeks. Obviously, his mother's machinations embarrassed her, too.

He stretched his neck, pretending to look for the man, who, of course, he hadn't seen at all. Instead of seeing him now, he spotted Miss Irvine across the room. She stole a glance around her, then slipped through a door onto the terrace.

*Meeting Charles for a tryst, no doubt*, he thought, clenching his teeth. He'd seen the look that had passed between the pair earlier, and he'd imagined he had detected a spark between them.

"There he goes now, I believe." He glanced back at Lady Louisa and bowed. "Have a lovely evening, my lady."

Her shoulders relaxed visibly. "You, too, your grace."

He hurried toward the door he'd seen Miss Irvine use, unsure what he intended to do. At the very least, he was going to see exactly what she and Charles were up to, assuming they hadn't disappeared into some undiscoverable part of the garden.

When he stepped onto the terrace, he found her almost immediately, alone at the rail, her back toward him. He stood in the shadows and watched her for a moment. Her pale hair, curled and pinned up elegantly, glowed in the moonlight. The nape of her neck curved gracefully, beckoning to be kissed. She wore a plain gown, even for such a grand occasion, but the simple lines of the fabric delineated the curves of her body to perfection. As she leaned forward on the rail, he had an excellent view of her slim waist and round bottom.

A longing welled up inside him to step up behind her and slide his arms around her. He wished *he* was the one she was expecting to meet her.

Actually, she didn't appear to be expecting anyone.

He studied her for another moment. She never looked back at the house, instead gazing out at the garden or up at the moon. When he followed suit, he finally noticed that it was a gorgeous night—a romantic setting, in fact. Suppose he approached her before Charles arrived, if indeed Charles were coming at all. This could be an excellent chance to initiate his plan to divert her attentions toward him.

Cautiously, he took a step forward. He heard her murmur something, apparently not to anyone but herself.

Curious, he inched closer.

" '*. . . in such a night,*' " she said, " '*Troilus, methinks, mounted the Trojan walls and sighed his soul toward the Grecian tents where Cressid lay that night.*' "

Troilus and Cressida again? Suddenly he realized she was quoting from *The Merchant of Venice.* The words were from that magical scene between the young lovers in the play. Yes, it must have been a night like this that inspired Shakespeare when he wrote the scene.

He recited from just behind her, " '*In such a night as this, stood Dido with a willow in her hand upon the wild sea-banks, and waft her love to come home again to Carthage.'* "

She whirled around, her eyes large and round. "Your grace! You startled me."

"Forgive me." He grinned and stepped up beside her, leaning one hand on the rail. "I confess I got caught up in the drama of the scene—this beautiful night, Shakespeare's eloquent words . . . your lovely form."

Her eyes widened again. She swallowed and turned to face the garden again. "Well, you skipped one."

"I skipped one what?"

"An *'In such a night.'* " Her voice sounded breathless. "You skipped the Thisby and Pyramus lines."

He thought back on the play, then shrugged. "The Dido lines are better."

A moment of silence passed between them. Then a laugh escaped her. She covered her mouth and closed her eyes. "Every time I think I have you figured out, you say something entirely unexpected."

It was his turn to hesitate. "Yes, well, some of the things I say aren't well thought out. I'm sorry about our last encounter. My opinions came out sounding a bit more strong than perhaps they are."

She peered at him from the corner of her eyes. "When you stand here daring to shrug off Shakespeare's genius, I can hardly believe you're the same man who . . . who said those dark things. But in any case, I overreacted, too. Let's try to get past our differences."

"Agreed." He turned toward the garden as well, nudging closer to her so that his sleeve nearly touched her bare arm. Her hair smelled of rosewater. "Why are you out here all alone? You can't have run out of dance partners. I've seen you on the floor for every set."

A hint of distress flickered over her features. "I needed some air."

He frowned, remembering he'd seen his mother talking to her a while ago and had observed that Miss Irvine looked troubled. Several times since the duchess had told him of her attempt to counsel Miss Irvine, he had pictured the scene and cringed. Sometimes the woman's audacity mortified him.

"Has my mother been badgering you, by chance?" he asked.

"I've spoken very little with her grace this evening."

She had avoided his question, he noted. His mother's officiousness was getting intolerable. He didn't know how much longer he could take her pressing Lady Louisa upon him. Staring into the darkness, he said, "I wish I could say the same."

At last he felt her gaze upon his face. "Was the duchess badgering *you?"*

"No more so than usual. She is forever trying to . . . well, to press her favorites upon me." He glanced at her and looked away again, wondering if he should have said so much. Did he sound like a whining little boy? His mother's treatment forced him into a defensive position. Frustration surged inside him, and he could barely continue speaking. ". . . no matter how many times I assure her that her efforts are futile."

"You, too, have sworn off marriage?" Miss Irvine asked, her voice quavering.

"Yes," he said automatically.

She hesitated. "You really did love Belinda."

"Well . . . of course." The conversation was approaching dangerous waters. All at once he remembered he was supposed to be wooing her. "Actually, Miss Irvine, eschewing marriage was my inclination immediately after Belinda's death, but lately I do have moments when I'm no longer sure."

The truth of his words surprised him. When he

looked at her and their gazes locked, the moment felt intense. She searched his eyes, and he wondered what she saw in them. Something akin to apprehension?

She broke their shared stare and looked away. "Doubtlessly over the past couple of years you've considered many factors. Your daughter, for example."

"Yes." He frowned. He had indeed thought a lot about how the girl would be affected by her lack of a mother. "Eliza could benefit from having a female influence other than my mother in her life. Of course, Lady Blaine is here for her, too—but grandmothers have a different role from a mother."

Miss Irvine stood silent and very still.

He gave a short, nervous laugh. "Somehow the conversation has taken a very serious turn. What happened to Shakespeare and magical nights?"

Another moment passed. Then she set her hand on his arm, her touch light and tender.

He shot a look at her in surprise.

"You're right." She gave him a soft smile and tilted her head to one side. "'Tis a glorious evening. Why don't we do what we can to enjoy it? Is it true that you never dance?"

"I have not for many years."

Her smile puckered, drawing his gaze straight to her mouth. The pout was subtle, but it was there. The urge to wipe away the hint of wistfulness with a kiss overwhelmed him. He looked back into her eyes again, his gaze heated.

She returned his stare. The pout ebbed, and her lips parted slightly.

Tentatively, he reached to push back a loose lock of her hair from her face. She drew in her breath but made no move to resist his touch. Her cheek felt hot and baby-smooth against the tips of his fingers. She continued to hold his gaze, so he bent to kiss her . . . and he knew she was going to allow him.

"Adrian!" The duchess's shrill voice made both of them jump, pulling away from one another. "What on earth are you doing out here?"

He shot her a look, his eyes narrowing. Confound the woman, interfering at such a time! He was a grown man and would do whatever he pleased. Instead of honoring her demand with a response, he turned his back to her and stared out into the garden.

A few awkward seconds passed. Then Miss Irvine cleared her throat beside him. "I, er, may have had a foreign object in my eye, ma'am. An eyelash, perhaps. Your son kindly offered to help extract it."

Footsteps approached, to Adrian's disbelief. His mother had no concept of the bounds of her authority.

"Indeed?" she asked, her tone laced with sarcasm. "Would you not fare better if you made an attempt in the light?"

Adrian glanced over at Miss Irvine. She held her chin high and met his mother's gaze straight on. Her posture expressed what civility didn't allow her to say outright—that she would not be intimidated by the duchess's tactics. He admired her for refusing to cower.

"One might think so," she said, "and yet the eyelash isn't bothering me anymore. The duke must have dislodged it."

"How fortuitous. Perhaps you should return to the dance floor then. Your aunt is wondering where you are."

"If Aunt Eleanor is concerned, I shall certainly reassure her." She started toward the house.

Adrian spun around. "Wait, Miss Irvine."

She stopped and looked over at him.

"I believe this is our dance," he said.

Her eyebrows lifted just perceptibly, and she blinked

at him for a moment. The opening strains of a waltz drifted through the door onto the terrace.

He stepped up to her and took her hand. "I don't think Lady Blaine will mind if you wait to speak to her. Likely we can catch her eye from the dance floor."

A hint of a smile tugged at one corner of her mouth. She suppressed it by pursing her lips. Her look simulated censure, but she gave him a short nod of assent.

As he led her inside, he glanced back to his mother. "Please excuse us, ma'am."

Before she had time to react, he swept his partner through the door. Through the windows, he got one last glimpse of the duchess crossing her arms over her chest.

When they reached the dance floor, Miss Irvine let out a giggle. "I fear your mother is going to have much to say to you about this, your grace."

"On the contrary, I'm hoping it will teach her to know when to keep her opinions to herself."

He took her in his arms, careful to maintain a proper distance between them. Still, her proximity intoxicated him. Her waist felt impossibly slender, and the soft curve of her back beneath his hand drove him to distraction.

A trace of rosewater grazed his nose, and the light of a thousand candles whirled by to add to the headiness of the experience. His mind reeled with mixed emotions.

*She would have kissed me,* he thought, looking into her eyes. He had no doubt she would have—but *why* was another question. Did she view him as a quick way to financial security? He considered the context of the moment, their conversation about Belinda. Maybe Miss Irvine had simply pitied him, her cousin's poor widower.

Lady Blaine passed close to them in the arms of Lord Paterson. When she noticed Adrian with her niece, the startled expression on her face was almost comical. The next instant, she had breezed by.

Miss Irvine let out a throaty laugh. "Oh, dear. We are shocking all of our relatives, your grace."

The saucy grin she gave him reminded him of how she'd looked when they had first met on the docks. That day he had wondered if she had a wanton streak, as he had again the time she'd mentioned anatomy studies. Perhaps her willingness to kiss him was only evidence of a lack of moral fiber.

Gazing into her sparkling eyes, he almost didn't care what motivated her. One thing was certain: He wanted to kiss her now more than ever. He longed to waltz her back out onto the terrace and finish what he'd started, to see if she responded the way he hoped.

The move wouldn't be wise, however. He didn't have to look around the room to know how much attention his return to the dance floor had garnered. He could feel the focus of eyes from every corner. The brief instant of privacy he and Miss Irvine had shared was lost.

But it wouldn't be the last. They were family. He had countless opportunities to be alone with her. The thought made his blood quicken. He didn't want to wait.

"Are you still interested in visiting a museum with me this week?" he asked her.

She smiled again. "Of course, if you can find the time."

"How about tomorrow afternoon? Perhaps we could see Elgin's Marbles."

Her grin widened. "Even if I had plans, I'd cancel them for Elgin's Marbles. Fortunately, I'm free."

"Perfect. I'll come by to collect you shortly after noon."

With the engagement established, he figured he'd accomplished enough for the evening. Much seemed to have happened in a small stretch of time, and he needed time to absorb it all. He said very little for the remainder of the set, using the time to compose himself.

When the music ended, he spotted Lady Blaine walking off the floor, still chatting with her partner. He guided Miss Irvine toward them and thanked her for the dance.

"My pleasure," she said.

Her smile, he thought, looked a bit reserved, as if she too had spent the last few minutes reexamining the situation and dampening her demeanor.

Though Lady Blaine and her partner appeared embroiled in conversation, Adrian left Miss Irvine with them. He meant to get to the card room as quickly as possible, before any ambitious mothers in the room got the idea that he might dance with their daughters if pressed.

As he reached the archway leading to the room, he paused for one last glance back at Miss Irvine. To his annoyance, he saw Charles approaching her. His cousin greeted her with a lopsided grin that positively exuded mischief.

The duke frowned.

Miss Irvine smiled and appeared comfortable with the young fop, even when Charles leaned close to her ear and whispered something.

*What can he possibly have to say to her that can't be heard by anyone present?* he wondered.

She nodded slowly and responded, her expression filled with interest. Any observer would have thought they had a matter of substance to discuss rather than simply small talk.

Adrian watched for another minute until Lady Blaine parted from her companion and joined their conversation. With his mother-in-law present, he felt reasonably confident they weren't planning how to spend his money when he kicked off.

Finally, he turned into the card room. He walked to a table in the rear and stood back, observing the play—or trying to. His mind kept straying to the ballroom. Was Charles still leaning close to Maeve Irvine? Dancing with her? Talking her into cancelling the trip to see Elgin's Marbles tomorrow so she could do something with him?

In the end he grew so restless, he went to the archway to find out. No one stood where he had last seen them. He surveyed the room and spotted Miss Irvine dancing with an older, balding man, who made several missteps as he watched.

Ducking back inside the card room, Adrian put a hand up to knead his brow. He hadn't been so preoccupied with a female since his young bachelor days. It was nerve-racking, but he had to admit it was also stimulating.

He took a deep breath and lifted his face. It seemed he was back among the living.

# Eight

The following morning Maeve woke near her normal hour. Immediately, memories of the previous evening flooded her head. The duke had nearly kissed her—if she wasn't mistaken. She'd lain awake half the night trying to decide if she could be mistaken, and she didn't believe she was.

She rolled over on her side. Why in heaven's name had he thought to kiss her? She couldn't put it down to a whim, because it hadn't been a frivolous moment. They'd been talking about his vow against marriage. Then he noted that lately he'd had second thoughts about it. From what she could glean from him, Eliza was the reason he'd backed down from his strong stance. He believed the child needed a mother.

Just after confiding that, he had attempted the kiss. She could only surmise that he thought she—his late wife's cousin—would make an appropriate stand-in.

She drew in a long breath. The idea frightened her—and tantalized her just a little. After the previous night, she could no longer deny how much the duke attracted her. Dancing with him would have been exciting enough, but it was the encounter in the garden that truly left her reeling. If his mother hadn't interrupted, she would have let him kiss her.

If he made her an offer—for the sake of her own

cousin's child—would she reconsider her own views of marriage?

Putting her hands to her cheeks, she tried to calm herself. 'Twas all too much to think about. She barely knew the man. What if he tried to discuss the plan during their outing today?

She sat up in bed, now twice as agitated, but she had to admit she still looked forward to the outing. If he tried to broach any topic she wasn't prepared to discuss, she'd simply have to tell him she needed time to think.

Unable to settle her thoughts, she rose and got dressed.

When she arrived downstairs, she found the breakfast room empty, as she had expected. Aunt Eleanor had danced up a storm at the ball and had scarcely been able to keep her eyes open during the drive home. Considering her aunt's amazement over her dance with the duke, Maeve thanked her stars for the reprieve from excited questioning. It had been impossible to convince the woman that her son-in-law's gesture had been purely platonic. Though Maeve found his attempt to kiss her hard to understand, she knew he'd singled her out to dance merely to rankle his mother.

A young maid entered the room carrying a steaming teapot. "Good morning, Miss. I've brought your tea. You'll find the hot food is already waiting."

"Thank you." Realizing she'd been staring out the window, Maeve headed for the sideboard and dished herself a small serving of eggs.

The servant set down the pot and fussed with the table settings. Turning toward the kitchen, she paused. "Is there anything else you need, Miss?"

"Hmm? Oh, no, I'm fine."

As the woman left, Maeve added a croissant to her plate and took a seat at the table. The near kiss was haunting her again. If the duke was considering proposing a marriage of convenience, he didn't need to kiss her. Had he made the attempt out of politeness? Perhaps after their argument about *Troilus and Cressida,* he'd pegged her for a romantic and feared she wouldn't settle for pure convenience.

She frowned. If he was trying to look romantic simply because he thought she wanted it, the situation was rather embarrassing. She chewed slowly on her roll, her already small appetite dwindling.

"Good morning, dear."

The cheerful feminine voice made her look up as her aunt entered the room. Wearing a lemon-colored gown as vibrant as her smile, the countess went straight to the sideboard. As she made her breakfast selections, she chattered nonstop.

"What a ball last night." She uncovered a container of mixed grilled meats and picked up a pair of tongs. "I still can hardly credit that you got Adrian out on the floor. What in the world did you say to him?"

Maeve forced her focus on her aunt. "Oh, nothing at all. The waltz was his idea."

"*His idea?* Why, he's even more taken with you than I believed."

The sparks of hope glittering in the countess's eyes nearly made Maeve wince. "No, Auntie, you presume too much. During our conversation last night, he actually told me that after Belinda died, he vowed never to marry again."

"La, dear, a man will always claim he doesn't intend to marry." She added a piece of toast to her plate and came to the table. "How vexing that I couldn't find Jane at the end of the night. I'm dying to hear what she has to say about this."

Maeve's fork slipped through her fingers and clattered on her plate. "Oh, no, Aunt Eleanor, please. Even if there were something between the duke and me—and I assure you there isn't—I should feel very awkward if you discussed it with his mother."

Her aunt gave her a sly smile and nodded. "Very well. I suppose such talk *would* embarrass you. I promise to wait and see what develops before I say anything to Jane."

"Thank you—and please try not to form any unreasonable expectations."

"Oh, I never do that." She poured herself a cup of tea and set down the pot. "What are you wearing for your engagement with Adrian today?"

"I was going to wear this."

The countess glanced at Maeve's dress, a simple white muslin adorned with a smattering of sprigs. "Oh, come now, dear. Wear your striped sarcenet. The blue will bring out your eyes, and the gold your hair."

Maeve set down her cup and looked at her aunt. "When have you seen my striped sarcenet?"

"I ran into Miss Grey in the upstairs hall just now, and she called me into your room to show me. She already has the outfit pressed and laid out for you."

She frowned. Grey was up to her tricks again, and now she was enlisting help. "You know I'm trying to maintain the appearance of a poor relation."

"With Adrian? You can't possibly fear *he* is a fortune hunter. If you have any doubts, I can assure you his finances are perfectly healthy. Jane is a bit of a braggart, you know. I'm privy to specifics, if you want them."

"I have no interest in his finances!"

"Of course not, but my point is that you needn't pretend to be poor when you're with him. At least you needn't go to any great lengths." Aunt Eleanor looked at her with large, hopeful eyes. "So will you wear the sarcenet? You can tell him I bought it for you, if that helps."

All at once the absurdity of the situation struck Maeve. Her aunt and her abigail were practically begging her to wear a gown that had once been her favorite. She let out a laugh. To own up to the truth, she missed her sarcenet. She was tired of wearing the same five old dresses over and over since she had left Boston. "Very well, Auntie. You win. I'll go to Grey as soon as I'm finished eating."

"Excellent." The countess gave her a broad grin. "You won't regret it."

Once Maeve had changed clothes and allowed Grey to arrange her hair, she had to admit she felt the better for it. Looking over her reflection in the mirror, she had a sense that she was seeing her old self, the person she had been before Thomas had abandoned her and made her doubt everything she'd once believed. A sudden urge came over her to drop her defenses and simply enjoy her day out.

*Is it possible?* she wondered, studying her face in the glass. Could she, for once, keep the conversation light between her and the duke? Could she trade banter with him as she had the first time they'd met, maybe even hope he would make another attempt to steal a kiss?

She raised her eyebrows at herself. Perhaps that last thought was taking things too far, but she did deserve a day of enjoyment after all this time, did she not? Yes, she did!

Smiling, she turned away from the mirror. As she picked up her reticule, she felt young again. She felt alive.

Adrian's ride to South Audley Street passed quickly—too quickly for him to decide upon the best way to treat Miss Irvine during their excursion. He definitely wanted to further their acquaintance. Yes, in fact, he wanted to flirt with her—but he couldn't help being nervous. It was if he were a schoolboy in pursuit of his first love, instead of a widowed man attempting to protect his family from an adventuress.

What reason did he have for apprehension? Did he fear he'd fall prey to her machinations? Surely he was past getting entangled with the wrong sort of woman merely because she was beautiful. He had learned his lesson with Belinda.

When he stood looking up at Lady Blaine's house, he was still wary. Swallowing his qualms, he walked up to the door and dropped the knocker.

The butler admitted him without delay. As he entered, the countess herself glided down the main staircase.

"Good morning, Adrian. Thank you for taking my niece out today." She glanced past his shoulder at the servant closing the door, then focused on him again. "I'd hoped your mother might tag along and visit for a while. I barely saw her last night, or indeed these past few days."

"Really?" The news surprised him, but in fact he hadn't given the duchess an opportunity to accompany him today. He'd seen her only in passing, and they had barely wished each other good morning. "I believe she's been somewhat preoccupied. She seemed so today."

"I see. Well, I hope whatever's troubling her will soon be resolved. Please tell her I asked after her." His hostess walked to the double doors to his left and opened them. "Come into the drawing room, Adrian. Maeve will be down in a moment."

He followed her through, and she sat down in her usual chair. He went to the settee across from her, but as he sat, he noticed a large leatherbound book beside him.

"Oh, Maeve must have left her sketchbook lying about again," Lady Blaine said, noticing where his gaze had wandered. "Do take a look, Adrian. You won't believe how talented she is."

He would have loved to pick up the book and skim through it, but he remembered that Miss Irvine had once denied him the privilege. Nevertheless, he couldn't resist peeking at the open page. A drawing of a man's handsome face, meticulously executed in charcoal, stared up at him with dark, fathomless eyes. Who was he? A lover of hers from back in America? He felt a sick stirring in his stomach.

"Maeve drew that one from the portrait of my father that hangs in the library," Lady Blaine said. "Don't ask me how, but she managed a better likeness than the original painter. Perhaps she has some sort of innate sense of her grandfather's character that she captured on paper."

He looked more closely at the drawing and now remembered the face. Lady Blaine was correct. The portrait in the library lacked the lifelike quality of this one. "Well, I never knew the man, but when I look into these eyes, I feel as though I do."

"Maeve says she drew it to become acquainted with him. Judging from the result, I daresay her plan worked. She had never seen his likeness before coming to London."

He studied the portrait for another moment. Then the sound of footsteps made him look up to see the artist herself arrive. She looked stunning in a fashionable gown and spencer that hugged her lithe figure. Just as he was wondering who had paid for it, she spotted the book and rushed to the settee to grab it.

"Auntie, I told you not to let anyone see this. You know some of the drawings are . . . er, personal." She snapped the book shut and stashed it inside a nearby cabinet. Turning to Adrian, she said, "I'm sorry, your grace. Perhaps another time."

Recalling his manners, he stood and bowed. "As you wish, but you did say you'd show me the book when we knew each other better. Are we not better acquainted now?"

She gave him a crooked smile. "Not quite well enough, your grace."

"But perhaps well enough that you could call me Adrian?"

An unexpected hint of pink tinged her cheeks. "I confess that I've begun to think of you as Adrian. Aunt Eleanor always calls you that, of course. Yes, let's dispense with titles. Please call me Maeve."

"About time," Lady Blaine said, beaming. "We are all family, after all."

Adrian stepped closer to Maeve, pleased at this progress toward familiarity. "The sketch of your grandfather is superb, by the way. You possess a unique talent for capturing lifelike detail."

She laughed. "Kind of you to say, but wait till we see Elgin's Marbles. From what I've read, the statues are so lifelike that one expects them to move at any moment. I cannot tell you how excited I am in anticipation."

He stared at her, noting that her entire face seem to glow. "I'm excited, too."

*A damned sight too excited,* he thought, hearing the huskiness in his voice. But he had a good reason to flirt, so curbing his attraction to her would be counterproductive. It wasn't as though he didn't have his wits about him. He wasn't in love with her, only trying to learn more about her.

"Is something wrong, Adrian?" Lady Blaine asked. "You have a frown on your face."

"No, nothing." He turned toward his mother-in-law. "I was only trying to remember something—something about the estate accounts."

"Oh, pooh," she said. "Forget the estate accounts today."

"Definitely," Maeve said. "Don't let anything distract you from the art of the ancients. For this special occasion, you must think only of beauty and light."

His gaze shot back to her and slipped to her lips. "A tempting proposition."

"The only kind worth indulging." She took his arm and looked to the countess. "I'll see you this afternoon, Auntie. We'll try not to linger too long at the museum."

"Take your time, dear. I'm used to keeping myself occupied, and I know you'll be in safe hands." She smiled at Adrian, and he felt a pang a guilt that he planned a bit of a dalliance with the woman his mother-in-law was entrusting to his care.

They finished their good-byes, and Maeve tugged gently on his arm all through the front hall and outside. Glancing up at him on the front steps, she said, "Please forgive me for being so eager. I've never experienced anything like this. Museums in the States are rare, and the ones I've visited boast very few antiquities."

As they stepped into the sunlight, her eyes sparkled, and Adrian felt her enthusiasm spreading to him. "You make me feel rather jaded, as though I've never fully appreciated the cultural advantages I have."

"Well, when one has always had advantages, one tends to take them for granted." She stopped in front of his barouche, shielding her eyes from the sun. "May we ride on the box? It's such a lovely day."

"If you like."

She tossed her reticule up onto the bench and placed one foot on the first step. Adrian stepped forward to offer her his hand but realized how little help the gesture would provide for such a steep climb. Acting on impulse, he grasped her slim waist with both hands and lifted her up with ease. As she found footing on the platform, he let his hands slide down, just grazing the delicious curve of her hips.

"Thank you," she said, barely meeting his gaze before she looked away. Pick infused her cheeks, and he wondered if his touch or her effort had caused her heightened coloring.

"My pleasure." He strode around to the opposite side of the carriage and climbed aboard.

"My father once took me to the Peale Museum in Philadelphia," she said as he joined her on the box. "We saw the bones of a most extraordinary creature called a mastodon. Have you ever heard of such a thing?"

"I don't believe so." He took up the reins and urged the horses off into a trot. "What makes the creature extraordinary?"

"Why, it's huge! Much like an elephant, only larger. And no one has ever found a living example. Papa told me that Mr. Charles Peale suspects the animals no longer exist, though many find his theory heretical."

"Interesting." Adrian noted that until now she had never spoken to him about her life in America. If he inquired about her upbringing, perhaps he could get a better idea of her character. "Did you and your father make many such trips to museums?"

"There weren't many museums to visit." She watched the passing city scenery as she spoke. "But Papa was a man of diverse interests, and he did all he could to whet my appetite for cultural pursuits. Though he didn't draw himself, he encouraged my efforts from the time I was a child."

"His encouragement paid off. And what about your mother? What was she like?"

"I'm afraid I can't tell you much about her. She died when I was too young to know her."

*Ah, a loss that, unfortunately, might have led to defects in her character.* He glanced at her profile and felt a tug of sympathy. "I'm sorry. You must have felt her absence keenly."

"Very much at times. Not that I lacked parental affection. My father was wonderfully attentive." She looked down into her lap. "I daresay, however, that I could have used a stronger feminine influence in my life than my governess and godmother could provide."

Unsure how to respond, he took a moment to think. He suspected she'd suffered some deficiency in the way she was raised, but he couldn't very well tell her so. He chose to sidestep the issue. "I wouldn't say you lack femininity. No one could call you a hoyden."

"But perhaps I'm rather too brazen at times?" She looked him in the eye, as though she dared him to answer truthfully.

The question itself was rather brazen. He met her steady gaze. Suddenly he realized how much courage she possessed. Even if her motives for coming to England proved less than noble, making a transatlantic move took courage.

"Perhaps more brave than brazen." He looked back to the horses as he guided them around a bend. "It took courage to pack up and move to England. Even if . . . if your father's death left you in financial straits, surely it would have been easier to find a way to get by at home than to start a whole new life here."

A moment of silence ensued. He peeked at her out of the corner of his eye and saw her frowning to herself.

"Maybe brave moves are easier to make when one is desperate," she said at last. "Money isn't the only thing a person needs to live. When I decided to come to Aunt Eleanor, I really needed family."

"You didn't have friends close enough to step in for your family?"

"Miss Grey, my abigail, has always been my closest companion, and she moved here with me, of course. Some others whom I considered close . . . well, let's just say no, they did not step in for my family." At that moment, they reached their destination, and she looked up at the museum as they pulled to the side of the road. "Ah, here we are! I can't wait to get inside and pretend I'm walking in ancient Greece."

He wanted to ask more about her past, but to press her further would have been intrusive. Clearly, someone close to her had failed her. Perhaps the experience had made her cynical enough to concoct a scheme to prey on a rich relation. He wondered if after meeting her aunt in person she'd had second thoughts. The two seemed genuinely fond of one another. Was that why Maeve had started up a flirtation with Charles, to refocus her schemes on a different target? Would she just easily turn her sights on a wealthy duke who showed interest in her?

As they entered the museum, he still hoped to renew his questioning, but her excitement over the art on display made it impossible to introduce other topics. When they reached Elgin's Marbles themselves, the lifelike detail of the sculptures enraptured him, as well. The thought of discussing anything else flew from his mind.

"Oh, my goodness." She stopped in front of a portrayal of Herakles and clapped one hand over her chest. The ancient god lounged gracefully against a boulder, his muscular nude body stretched out in a manner that would shock most young women. Maeve, however, sucked in her breath and leaned in close to him, obviously feeling nothing but reverence.

The work was masterful, but Adrian eyed the onlooker with more interest. Perhaps as a student of art, she had seen male nudes before. Or perhaps she had another, less innocent reason to be comfortably familiar with the male body. . . .

"Oh, Adrian," she breathed. "I would swear that blood flows within that stone flesh. I *have* to touch him."

His jaw went slack as she placed one hand on the god's bare shoulder and ran her fingers over his perfectly formed biceps. He couldn't help but imagine her fingers caressing his own body the same way. "Maeve, do you really think you should . . ."

Her hand dropped to the statue's muscular thigh, slowly tracing a line down to the gracefully jutting bones of the knee. "It's *hard*, Adrian. So like flesh, yet it truly is stone."

He swallowed. A stirring in his groin threatened to make a spectacle of him if he failed to steer his thoughts elsewhere.

She glanced at him and must have read his discomfort in his expression. "Ah, I gather that British propriety is rearing its formidable head again. You disapprove of my touching an ancient artifact. Must you go all rigid on me now, like a marble statue yourself?"

Fixing his gaze firmly on her face, he tried to smile, but managed only a grimace. "I shall do all I can to prevent it."

As she looked back down at Herakles, he drew in a long breath, turned, and walked across the room, ostensibly to view another statue.

For the remainder of their visit, he concentrated on watching the art and not his companion. She seemed not to notice, completely caught up in wonder over the statues.

On the ride home, she overflowed with observations about what they'd seen, and he did his best to comment with some intelligence. At last, as they drove into South

Audley Street, he slipped in one more personal question about her.

"Last night on the terrace I noticed you were reciting lines about Cressida, and the last time we spoke of her story you seemed very sympathetic toward her. Is there some affinity you have for her?"

Her lively expression went bland. She looked straight ahead, but not at the street—far into the distance. "I *am* Cressida."

Though he should have been prepared for any response she made, a sick lump formed in his gut. She had as good as admitted to being an unfaithful lover. The only matter left to question was the extent of her vices. "What do you mean?"

She sighed and brought her somber gaze up to meet his. "Part of me longs to unburden my mind and tell you all, but another part is reluctant. I'm afraid I'd rather save the story for another time. This day has been so perfect, I'd hate to spoil it."

He could see pain in her eyes, and another pang of compassion stabbed him. Earlier she'd hinted that someone she had loved had failed her. Had it been a suitor, whom she had then betrayed in retaliation? If she told him the whole story, would he condemn her or not? He was dying to know more, but he didn't want to add to her pain with impertinent questions.

He reached out and touched her cheek. "I don't want to spoil it, either."

She froze.

Their gazes locked, and he knew she was thinking of the previous evening, of the moment when they'd both known he was about to kiss her.

He let his gaze sink to her lips, full and slightly parted. Although he hadn't decided how far he should take his flirtation, temptation took over. Cupping her cheek, he leaned forward and met her mouth. Her lips were warm and soft and delicious. The scent of rosewater teased his nose, adding to the headiness of the moment.

A quiet moan escaped her throat and nearly drove him wild. He deepened the kiss, and she let him taste her tongue. The urge seized him to wrap his arms around her and fall to the bench entangled with her.

Then he recalled that they were in full public view.

With great force of will, he pulled apart from her. He darted looks up and down the street. No one appeared to be watching.

He turned back to her and swallowed. "Forgive me. I . . . I'm appalled by my lack of judgment. No one saw, I think—but that doesn't lessen my culpability."

She pushed a stray lock of her hair behind her ear and cast her gaze downward. Her cheeks flushed and her eyes bright, she appeared as ready for lovemaking as he. She cleared her throat. "Some of the culpability is mine, I fear. I could have prevented this. I . . . I'd better go inside."

She turned away from him and started to rise.

"Wait—let me help you." He jumped down from the box and dashed around to her side of the carriage. To his surprise, she did as he asked instead of leaping down and running into the house before he could reach her. Looking up at her, he held out his hand.

She met his gaze and surprised him again by breaking into a tiny, crooked smile. Her eyebrows tilted upward, giving her an expression of embarrassed helplessness, a pleasant alternative to the mortified hauteur he had expected.

Relief flooded his body, and he smiled, too. She looked down, but she took his hand. Her fingers felt small and fragile. Once she'd reached the ground safely, he let them slip from his, and they walked to the house in silence.

At the door, she paused and turned to him. "Would you like to come inside? That is, Aunt Eleanor would like to spend more time with you, I'm sure."

He shook his head, doubting he would be able to act naturally in front of his mother-in-law after what had just transpired.

"She'll be disappointed," Maeve said, her voice still breathless.

A thought occurred to him. "My mother mentioned something about attending the opera Monday night. Perhaps you and Lady Blaine could join us in our box?"

She raised an eyebrow but hesitated only for a second. "My aunt is eager to see the duchess. I'm sure she'll want to go. Thank you for the invitation."

"Mother and I will pick you up on our way."

"How kind of you—and thank you for today, too. The day was definitely the highlight of my time in England so far. I mean, seeing Elgin's Marbles and all." She looked downward and blushed.

He couldn't help but grin. For him, the kiss had by far outshone viewing the artwork. The thought of the passion that little moan of hers had betrayed still made his blood quicken. It wasn't the first time she'd been kissed, he realized, judging by the way she had responded. His grin faded. "Yes, it was . . . an interesting day."

"Well, until Monday evening then." She gave him an abrupt curtsy and reached for the door handle.

"Maeve?"

When she looked back, he wasn't sure what he had intended to say. Impatience filled him to dispel his fears about her, to give in to his inclination to like her. He wished he knew whether or not he could trust in her essential goodness . . . but he didn't.

He took a deep breath. "You said you came here because you wanted to have family again."

She searched his eyes and tilted her head, her expression one of confusion. "Yes, I did."

*Where am I going with this?* He wanted to ask if she had come to love her aunt, but the question would no doubt seem bizarre to her. Instead he said, "I hope you'll find everything you wanted here—more, in fact."

She blinked at him. Emotion flickered across her features, only to dispel quickly. For a long moment, she appeared unable to respond. At last, she murmured, "A generous wish, I'm sure. Allow me time, if you will. My thanks again."

Before he could utter another word, she ducked into the house. He stood staring at the door, left to wonder exactly what feelings she had hidden from him.

Shuffling back to the carriage, he longed to know who she really was. *I am Cressida,* she had said. That statement alone should have cured any romantic interest he had in her. But there was more to her story. She'd been hurt by a suitor—or, perhaps, by a lover. The image of her stroking Herakles's thigh flashed through his mind.

Was she a wounded innocent or a practiced jade?

# Nine

Maeve escaped into the house and shut the door. She slumped back against the oak panels, her heart thumping wildly. Adrian wanted to marry her! He had kissed her and hinted about her gaining a family. Surely he referred to the ready-made daughter she would have if they married.

She put her hands up to her cheeks, still hot with excitement. His kiss had nearly made her swoon with dizzy pleasure. None of the brief kisses Thomas had stolen during their betrothal had ever taken over her senses like this one. And, still, Adrian had maintained control. How mortifying that he, instead of she, had been the one to stop the kiss! She had no illusion that he was in love with her. The marriage he had in mind was more one of convenience—not chaste, apparently, but certainly not a love match.

Stepping away from the door, she sucked in her breath. Perhaps that sort of marriage was what she needed, one without the high expectations of love.

But *could* she keep from falling in love with Adrian? The way his kiss had affected her made her doubt it.

For the next two days she tried to immerse herself in working on Mr. Leight's portrait, but she mulled over the same thoughts again and again. The prospect of being hurt again frightened her, but she did like the idea of mothering little Eliza—and possibly her own children as well. When she had sworn off marriage, letting go of her dreams of having children had been the hardest part.

Still, she was so afraid of her attraction to Adrian. He had deserted poor Belinda while she was pregnant with Eliza.

*Will he also leave me stranded just when I most need him?* Maeve wondered.

On Monday evening, when the time came to dress for the opera, she allowed Miss Grey to talk her into wearing another fine gown. This time they chose a low-cut cream-colored silk confection trimmed with gold filigree. The dress was among the most expensive Maeve owned, but she couldn't resist the temptation to look her best for Adrian, regardless of her doubts.

"Your cheeks are so pretty and pink tonight, Miss," the abigail said as she pinned up Maeve's hair. "You must be keen to see this opera you're attending."

In truth she didn't even know what opera was being staged, but she didn't want to let Miss Grey know the real reason for her excitement. "I've never before attended an opera. Father always said he didn't enjoy them."

"Yet *you* are eager to see one?" Miss Grey asked.

"Yes." Maeve moistened her lips. "You know how curious I am about new things."

The maid lifted one eyebrow. "Well, I suppose an opera is similar to a play, only set to music. Knowing how fond you are of plays, I daresay you will enjoy tonight. You loved that story of—of Cressy and her beau."

"Cressida?" Maeve winced as a hairpin jabbed her ear. The recurring discussions of Cressida were beginning to tire her. "Actually, although the character did intrigue me at first, I have to wonder why she couldn't have exercised more restraint. If she had withheld her regard for Troilus a bit longer, he never would have had the chance to spurn her."

"But she wouldn't have had that magical night with him either, Miss." Grey took another pin from a small table beside her. "Remember how she said it was too short?"

"Yes, *'Night hath been too brief.'* " Maeve sighed, wondering if Adrian would kiss her again this evening. Unfortunately, even if they married, she doubted he would ever give himself to her for an entire night.

*What a shocking thought!* Checking that line of thinking, she said, "Today's world certainly has its share of Troiluses, but where does one meet a man such as Paris? Not that I would want a war fought for me, Grey, but it would be nice to find a man who would make *some* effort, instead of dropping a woman the minute an easier option comes along."

"Do you reckon the duke might be the Paris sort?"

Maeve shot a startled look over her shoulder at the woman. "Why on earth would *he* come to mind?"

"The word downstairs is that he's spent years pining for his late wife." Miss Grey lifted a long gold ribbon from the vanity and began threading it through her mistress's hair. "They say he barely set foot in public until this spring, when he had to come to London on business. All the parlor maids call him a *romantic.*"

Maeve sniffed and turned back to the glass. "A lot of good being a romantic is when the object of one's affections has been dead for two years."

"I don't know." A hint of a smile played on the abigail's thin face. "Seems to me that the duke's late wife isn't the only woman on his mind these days. He's been at *your* heels ever since we stepped off the boat from America."

Maeve's heart quickened at the suggestion, and she

frowned at the foolish brightness her reflected eyes radiated. "Now don't try planting seeds of nonsense in my mind, Grey. The duke himself has told me he swore off marriage after my cousin's death."

"Maybe Lady Blaine should have a talk with him then. That little girl of his needs a mama, and I reckon you'd be the perfect choice."

Maeve shot another look over her shoulder. "Don't you dare get my aunt involved with this, Grey. 'Tis no more her business than it is yours."

"Very well, Miss." The servant pursed her lips and tucked a straying curl back into her mistress's coif. "Your hair is all finished. Is there anything else you need?"

Maeve stood and smoothed down the skirt of her gown, trying to do the same with her nerves. The soft, shiny fabric of the dress felt cool and elegant and helped to soothe her. "No. That will be all."

The woman curtsied and turned toward the door.

"You did a lovely job with my hair, Grey," Maeve called after her. "Thank you."

"Yes, Miss." She hesitated, then gave her a small smile. "Enjoy yourself tonight."

Miss Grey vanished into the hall, and Maeve glanced into the mirror one last time. Seeing that she indeed looked her best lent her some comfort.

As she left the room, she heard her aunt greeting the duke below stairs.

"Your mother chose not to come again tonight?" the countess asked. "But it was her idea to attend the opera in the first place."

Maeve frowned. The duchess undoubtedly was avoiding *her,* but her absence was hurting Aunt Eleanor. Something had to be done to mend the situation . . . but what?

"Mother entreated me to extend her apologies,"

Adrian replied as Maeve started down the staircase. "She says her head has been pounding today, so badly that she would not have enjoyed tonight's music."

"Indeed?" Noticing Maeve descending, her aunt threw her a worried glance before looking back to the duke. "Jane so rarely suffers from headaches."

"I hope she recovers quickly," Maeve said as she joined them at the foot of the stairs. Privately she wondered if she needed to take matters into her own hands and speak to the duchess, but she dreaded the thought of facing the formidable woman. "Hello, Adrian."

"Maeve, you look lovely." He took her outstretched hand and pressed his lips to her skin, ousting all thoughts she had of his mother. "I hope you ladies won't mind having to make do with only me for company."

His gaze held hers as he let her hand slide slowly from his, and she held back a shudder of excitement. She did, however, allow herself a smile.

He smiled and eyed her for a moment longer, while she fought to control a wave of giddy pleasure. It wouldn't do to encourage him too openly when she wasn't sure she wanted him to make the offer he had alluded to.

With great effort, she looked away from him and vowed to avoid any undue physical contact with him that evening.

As they rode to the opera house, her aunt remained quiet, but Adrian had much to say about the other day's trip to view Elgin's Marbles. He marveled over their lifelike qualities and remarked that he had almost expected Herakles to respond when Maeve had touched him.

"Tell me," he teased her from across the dimly lit carriage, "were you testing him for signs of life?"

She giggled, relieved that he wasn't upbraiding her

for handling the antiquity. "You appeared so uneasy when I touched him that I expected *you* to jump rather than he. I'm surprised to hear that the Marbles affected you so strongly. You had so little to say at the exhibit. From what you tell me now, I think you must have felt all that I did."

"Even more, I daresay." His eyes sparkled.

"I don't see how you could have," she said, pleased by his good humor. If he were always this playful, she would have been in even greater danger of falling for him. She knew she should be putting up a wall of detachment to protect herself now, but how often did she get to trade carefree banter with a handsome duke? Surely the wall could wait a little longer. "I'm glad you managed to enjoy our visit despite my embarrassing you by handling the exhibits."

"Oh, I *especially* enjoyed your handling the exhibits."

His mischievous grin seemed to connote a hidden meaning. She suspected he might be alluding to the fact that she had touched a representation of the male body. Judging it best not to ask for clarification, she only laughed.

When she glanced over at her aunt, however, the countess's vacant stare out the window curtailed her humor. Again, she contemplated speaking to the duchess, as awkward as such an encounter would be. She couldn't have Aunt Eleanor unhappy on her account.

The carriage pulled up to the opera house, and they stepped out into the crowd. Adrian took her aunt on one arm and her on the other. As they made their way to the entrance, Maeve scanned the mass of faces milling outside the building. Broad smiles and glittering jewels lent their wearers extra sparkle. She caught whiffs of various perfumes—some heavy, some light and pleasing.

Through it all, however, the faint scent of sandalwood she detected on her escort appealed to her most.

Inside the opera house, she met with a whole new set of glittering sights. The flashy attire of the *demimonde* in the pit below the duke's box intrigued her even more than that of the privileged classes around her. Outshining everyone in the audience was the production itself. Illuminated by thousands of candles, the cast members, with their paint-exaggerated beauty and elaborate costumes, appeared larger than life.

"Do you understand Italian?" Adrian whispered to her shortly into the first scene. Few distractions could have lured her attention from the stage, but his head bent to hers drew her like a magnet.

"Only a word here and there." She leaned so close to him that her cheek nearly brushed his. Only when he had kissed her had they been closer. "I don't mind, however. The cascading phrases are enchanting in themselves."

"Yes, they are." He glanced at her lips before meeting her gaze with mesmerizing proximity.

Her jaw fell open slightly before she remembered herself and snapped it shut. Unless she was prepared to marry him, she had to stop behaving in such a besotted manner. She forced her gaze back to the stage and concentrated on the beautiful music ringing through the house.

When the curtain closed for the first intermission, she leaned forward to look around Adrian at her aunt. To her relief, the countess appeared more relaxed than she had earlier.

"The performance is marvelous, is it not?" Maeve asked, addressing both of her companions. "I wouldn't mind stretching my legs, however. Shall we go for a stroll?"

Adrian immediately began to rise, but Aunt Eleanor shook her head. "I'm not quite ready to brave those dreadful hordes again. Perhaps during the second break, dear, if you would be willing to wait."

"Of course," she said, though she felt a bit disappointed. She wanted to take in more of the glamorous crowd.

As Adrian sat down again, a light rap sounded on the door of the box. They turned around to see Lord Paterson and Colonel Westfall standing outside.

"Come in, gentlemen," Aunt Eleanor said, breaking into a smile. "What a pleasure to see you here."

"The pleasure is ours," Lord Paterson said, his gaze fixed on her.

The countess turned to Maeve. "If you still want your stroll, love, perhaps Adrian will take you while these gentlemen are here to keep me company."

Maeve looked at the duke, who nodded his agreement.

"Mind that you come back quickly," her aunt added. "Intermission won't last long."

Maeve leaped up, eager not only for her walk, but to clear the way for Lord Paterson to sit with her aunt. She even thought of asking the colonel to join her and Adrian but dismissed the scheme as too transparent. Seizing her escort's hand, she led him out of the box with a quick "pardon us" to the others.

"Why are we in such a hurry?" Adrian asked as they nudged their way through the throngs in the aisles. "Are you hoping to find a deserted terrace where we can recite Shakespeare?"

"Must you bring up such a mortifying moment?" she asked, slowing her pace. Suddenly she realized she was still holding his hand, and she moved her fingers to his arm. "One doesn't like to be discovered reciting verses to oneself."

"I only meant to tease you." He drew her arm closer. "You weren't really embarrassed, were you?"

"Not as embarrassed as when your mother found us out there," she said automatically. When she recalled that at that moment he'd been about to kiss her, her cheeks filled with heat. She looked downward. "I've made a bad impression on the duchess from the start, I'm afraid. Unfortunately, she seems to be avoiding Aunt Eleanor because of me."

"I doubt that." He hesitated. "Though Lady Blaine did mention that Mother has been remote."

They reached a bottleneck before the doors leading out of the theater, and the crowd pressed them even more tightly together. Concentrating hard, Maeve said, "Don't worry. I've decided to speak to your mother and try to mend the situation. I ought to have done so already, but, frankly, the duchess can be rather intimidating."

He frowned. "So I've observed over the years."

As they passed through the crowded doorway, the crush intensified. The crowd pushed Maeve sideways and she nearly lost her grip on his arm, but he grabbed her around the waist. They squeezed through the archway facing each other, their bodies pressed together.

Maeve sucked in a gulp of air and lay her palms against his chest, keenly aware of the hard muscle beneath them. She stared up into his eyes, secretly willing him to wrap his arms around her. An instant later they broke through into the less populated concourse, and their bodies separated.

She pulled her gaze away from his and cleared her throat. "Tomorrow I'll visit the duchess. I refuse to toady to her, but I shall do what I can to mend fences."

"Another example of your courage," he murmured.

He took her hand in his, his fingers warm and comforting. "I admire you for being willing to confront her. Not many people do. In fact, I don't as often as I ought to."

She knew she should have transferred her grasp to his arm again, but she couldn't seem to forego the pleasure of holding his hand.

"Perhaps we should head back to the box," she said, her voice breathless. "By the time we make our way through the crowd again, the opera will have resumed."

"As you wish." He gave her a grin that seemed to say *I know my touch is driving you wild.*

Despite her will to pull her hand from his, she still couldn't do it. The swirling hordes bumping into them and threatening to separate her from him were too convenient an excuse to cling to him.

*I'm lost to him,* she thought, half frightened, half relishing the experience. *I cannot resist him. If he makes his offer tonight, I will never manage to respond in a rational manner.*

When they reached their box, Lord Paterson and Colonel Westfall rose to give them back their seats.

"Please stay," Maeve said. "We can sit behind you."

"I wish we could," Lord Paterson said, "but my sister and her family are waiting for us in my box."

"Thank you for the invitation," Colonel Westfall added with a bow. He turned to Adrian. "Pray give my regards to your mother, your grace. I hope she is feeling more herself already."

As the men exited the box, Adrian finally released her hand, moving aside for them to pass.

"Miss Irvine," a male voice whispered at her ear.

She spun around to see Charles Leight beside her.

"Hello, Charles," her aunt called from her seat, beaming. "Are you joining us?"

"Lady Blaine." He bowed to her and then to his

cousin. "I'm afraid I can't stay. Another party is expecting me, and I've only just arrived. I just need a quick word with Miss Irvine."

He pulled Maeve a step away from the box. She noticed the duke frowning at them and thought once again that Mr. Leight's manners were not all they could be.

"I've been very busy," the young man whispered, "but I wanted to make another appointment to sit for you. Pamela's ball is approaching, and I'm beginning to fear the portrait won't be finished in time."

" 'Tis almost complete," she said. "When is the ball?"

"This weekend." He looked at her with wide eyes.

"Well, I've been painting every day. I only need you to pose one last time, so I can adjust a few details. You'd better come for a sitting tomorrow. I'm free all day."

He nodded. "I'll make sure to be there in the morning."

"I believe I can finish the portrait in time, but the oils won't be dry. You'll need to take care when you present it."

"Of course! Thank you, Miss Irvine. I can't tell you how much I appreciate your help." Barely waving farewell to the others, he scurried away.

She reentered the box, embarrassed on behalf on him.

"What was that all about?" Adrian asked, his curt address revealing his annoyance.

"He wanted to set up a time for—" She stopped herself, remembering that the portrait was a secret. "Er, that is, he asked me if I wanted to . . . to go sightseeing tomorrow."

He frowned. "You seem somewhat uncertain about his invitation. Where does he propose to take you?"

"Er, well, he wasn't specific."

"In that case, I presume you didn't accept him."

She swallowed, taken off guard by his obvious disapproval. "Well, yes, I did."

A vein appeared on his temple. "You will allow a strange man to take you wherever he pleases?"

Aunt Eleanor leaned forward in her chair to look around him. "What is all this fuss about, Adrian? Charles is family, after all. When he escorts Maeve I have no more fear of his treating her dishonorably than I do when you take her on an outing."

His jaw dropped. For a moment he stared at the countess, clearly trying to assess whether or not she knew that he had kissed Maeve. He glanced at Maeve, then back to her aunt again, steeling his expression. Rising, he said, "Excuse me, ladies."

Before either of them could speak, he left the box and strode up the aisle. As if on cue, the orchestra began playing, and the audience hushed as the curtain rose.

Maeve looked over at her aunt, who stared back at her. The countess motioned for her to move into the seat Adrian had vacated. Still stunned, Maeve did as she suggested.

"See what trouble secrets start," her aunt said. "I never should have allowed Charles to talk you into painting this secret portrait for him."

"I don't understand why Adrian is so angry." Maeve glanced over her shoulder to look up the aisle, but he wasn't in sight. "He is rather a stickler, isn't he? Would it really be so reprehensible of me to accept a nonspecific sightseeing invitation?"

Aunt Eleanor laughed. "Silly goose! You've missed the point. Adrian is jealous of Charles."

Maeve's gaze shot to meet hers. For an instant her heart fluttered with excitement—but, no, she refused to set herself up for disappointment. A man who had twice left his wife to go to war voluntarily was not a man susceptible to jealousy. She looked away. "No, he only disapproves of my association with Mr. Leight. I daresay the young man's ill manners are reason enough for Adrian to find fault with him."

"Are they reason enough for him to stalk off from our box?"

She shook her head. "He can be very distant. You and I both know that."

The look of amusement on her aunt's face faded. She clearly comprehended that Maeve referred to his desertion of Belinda.

*I never should have said that,* she thought.

Aunt Eleanor looked her in the eye, her expression serious. "Only when he has good reason to be, I think."

"Hush," someone in the box behind them urged.

Maeve shrank in her seat, not daring to continue the conversation anyway. Her aunt's last statement confused her. Had the countess not understood her reference after all, or did she truly absolve her son-in-law of neglecting her daughter? She had once mentioned how spoiled Belinda had been. Did Aunt Eleanor actually blame *her* for Adrian's desertion?

The music rose in a particularly loud crescendo and pulled her gaze toward the stage. *I'm missing the opera,* she thought. She tried to focus on the production again, but her mind continued to wander. When would Adrian return to their box? How disgusted with her was he? If Mr. Leight was unacceptable, shouldn't he rather than she have borne the brunt of the duke's displeasure?

Perhaps Adrian had gone to find Mr. Leight and chastise him. The thought gave her some hope that she wasn't the true object of his wrath. She sat back in her seat. For the remainder of the act, she fared a little better at attending to the opera.

After the curtain closed for the second intermission, she scanned the crowd for several minutes, wondering where Adrian had gone. She was just about to comment to her aunt on his continued absence when she spotted him entering a box on the opposite side of the theater. An attractive woman clung to his elbow. When she turned, Maeve recognized her as Lady Louisa Postlethwaite. Adrian held the box door open for the debutante and greeted her family with a smile.

Maeve stiffened. So much for the theory that he'd left her and Aunt Eleanor to dress down Mr. Leight!

"Where do you suppose Adrian is?" her aunt asked.

"He's over there with the Postlethwaites," she said through clenched teeth.

Aunt Eleanor looked across the theater, squinting. "Ah, so he is. Well, he doesn't appear angry anymore. Perhaps he'll return to our box at the end of intermission."

Maeve watched for another moment as Lady Louisa gazed up at him with obvious admiration. "Not likely, when he has found a beautiful debutante to hang on his every word. We'll be fortunate if he gives us a ride home."

"La, Maeve, now I believe *you* are jealous."

She glanced over to see her aunt grinning at her. "Ha. I'm merely offended that he has stranded us here. Some escort! And he presumes to criticize Mr. Leight for his manners."

The countess let out a chuckle. She lifted her opera glasses and looked across the auditorium. "He's leaving the Postlethwaites' box now. See, Maeve? He was merely being polite, because Lady Louisa is a favorite of Jane's."

*Yes—unlike me.* Maeve crossed her arms over her chest. She knew she was behaving with suspicious petulance, but she couldn't seem to quell her emotions. Her aunt was dead right. She was jealous. The realization brought a lump to her throat. Her feelings for Adrian had already gone too far.

A moment later he appeared in the box.

"Pardon my absence." He bowed to each of them and took the seat Maeve had originally occupied. Facing forward, he didn't meet the gaze of either of his companions.

"Did you speak to Charles?" Aunt Eleanor asked.

His gaze darted to her. "What do you mean?"

"Didn't you go after him to find out where he intends to take Maeve tomorrow? You seemed concerned about the matter. I assumed that as the head of the family you had gone to speak to him."

He frowned and looked toward the stage again. "I didn't see Charles anywhere. Likely the party waiting for him is seated among the demimonde in the pits."

"Adrian! Such a remark is unfit in mixed company, especially with an unmarried lady present."

He twisted his mouth and glanced at Maeve from the corner of his eyes. "Pardon me."

She nodded, but he had already looked away.

After a moment of awkward silence, he turned back to her. "If you are at all uncomfortable about your engagement with Charles, I can come by tomorrow morning and speak to him before he takes you out."

"No," she said quickly, concerned about giving away her patron's secret. "That is, it won't be necessary. I'm quite comfortable with Mr. Leight."

One corner of his mouth turned downward, plainly revealing his disapproval.

Aunt Eleanor cleared her throat. "*I* will question Charles. You may rest assured that he won't take my niece anywhere without first informing me."

"Should you not be acting as chaperon?" Adrian asked.

She smiled. "Maeve is not a debutante. I didn't tag

along for your excursion with her, and I shan't get in Charles's way either."

He eyed her for a moment, then looked ahead and leaned back in his chair.

Maeve flashed her aunt a look of gratitude. She wished she herself had thought to say they would question Charles. Then perhaps Adrian would have judged her less reckless.

Unfortunately, she hadn't, and he sat stone-faced for the rest of intermission. During the final act, he never once leaned over to make a comment to her.

Worried about his regard, she lost track of the plot. How badly had this silly incident damaged her relationship with him? Suddenly it looked as though he had decided against making an offer to her.

She blinked rapidly to hold back tears. A heaviness in her heart made it all too clear that she had invested much hope in the duke. How could she have been so stupid? He was a man who had forsaken her cousin. He was a man who now condemned her merely for accepting—supposedly—an innocent invitation with his own cousin.

*I am better off without him,* she told herself, lifting her chin. Her quivering lower lip somewhat ruined the effect, but with determination she knew that she would steady it. She had weathered worse rejection in the past. Adrian was no more necessary to her happiness than Thomas had been.

Staring at the stage, she watched the rest of the production with no comprehension of the story. If some small part of her wasn't convinced all was well, she would make sure no one but she perceived it.

# Ten

Maeve's final session with Charles Leight proved one of the most difficult she'd ever endured. Between ruminating over the previous evening and fretting about visiting the duchess, she could barely concentrate on painting.

After about an hour, however, she had managed to get down the details she needed. She could add a few finishing touches later, once she had regained her composure.

Mr. Leight agreed to return in a day or two to get the portrait. While Maeve put away her paints, her aunt saw him to the door.

"Goodness," the countess said upon returning to the studio. "Are models always so fidgety?"

Maeve looked up from her box of supplies. "Was he fidgety? I didn't notice. Likely I wasn't much better than he today."

"Is something troubling you, dear?"

"I suppose the opera left me tired." She picked up a rag and wiped a streak of carmine red paint from her wrist. "I'd better learn how to disguise my mood for these sittings. If I don't develop a more entertaining personality, no one will want to pose for me."

"Forgive me for saying so, but that might not be a bad thing." Aunt Eleanor went to the chair where she'd been sitting and began packing her netting materials into a basket. "You know I don't like to see you catering to people's whims. You deserve to be indulged, not the other way around."

"I'd still rather do things for myself than have people toady to me because they have an ulterior motive."

Her aunt shot her a look. "Just remember that not everyone is as two-faced as that Thomas fellow you told me about. Adrian appears inclined to escort you to museums and the opera, and I'm sure he has no hidden agenda."

Maeve frowned. In actuality, he had only considered pursuing her because of his daughter, and now he seemed to have changed his mind. Not in the mood to contest the point, she removed her smock and brushed off the muslin gown underneath. "Are you still planning to go shopping with Great Aunt Lucinda today, or has Mr. Leight's visit exhausted you?"

The countess laughed. "On the contrary, after dealing with him, I truly need a shopping break. Are you certain you don't want to tag along?"

"Thank you again, but yes, I'm certain." Maeve looked away from her, wary of betraying her plan to sneak off and see the duchess. "I have some . . . correspondence to tend to."

Aunt Eleanor opened her reticule and fished out a pair of kid gloves. "Well, perhaps you won't be alone for long. I wouldn't be surprised if Adrian stops by."

Maeve would have laughed at the groundless optimism if she didn't feel like crying. She turned to a nearby escritoire and opened the top drawer, pulling out several sheets of stationery. "I believe the duke mentioned having some business with his banker this morning. Unless you have some specific reason to expect him here, I cannot imagine why he would call."

"Can you not?" The countess pursed her lips as she

pulled on her gloves. "From what I've seen, the two of you can scarcely tear yourselves apart. I noticed that you were holding hands when you returned after the first intermission last night."

"Did you also notice that we barely spoke to one another the rest of the evening?"

"Only because he was jealous of his cousin." Her aunt paused and tapped her chin in thought. " 'Tis true that he was a bit too sulky for his own good. I suppose he gets that from Jane. I can't for the life of me figure out what I've done to offend her, but I'm convinced she's dodging me."

"Oh, la." Avoiding her gaze, Maeve took out a bottle of ink and placed it beside the paper. "I'd wager that she rather than Adrian stops by today."

For a moment her aunt said nothing. Finally, she shrugged. "Well, I'm not going to worry about it today. In any case, I'd best be on my way. I hope you enjoy your solitude."

"Thank you." Maeve stepped forward and kissed her cheek. "Have a lovely shopping trip."

The countess smiled and tucked her reticule under one arm. "If, by chance, *someone* should call and you decide to go out, please leave word with Webster."

"In the unlikely event that someone does, I shall." She turned to the desk and picked up a quill.

"Au revoir, then. I promise I won't be gone long."

After her aunt had left the room, Maeve went to a front window and peered around the drapes until the carriage had pulled away from the house. She fetched her spencer and gloves and glanced up and down the main hall before ducking out the front door. Perhaps she ought to have told the butler where she meant to go and taken a maid for propriety's sake, but she didn't want news of her excursion to leak back to the countess through the servants.

Once outside, she closed the door softly and dashed down the steps. Too late she saw a man at the foot. As he caught her by the shoulders, preventing her from plowing into his chest, she recognized Colonel Westfall.

"Oh!" She struggled to regain her footing. "Pray pardon me, Colonel."

He let go of her and laughed. "Good day, Miss Irvine."

"Good day, sir. In my haste, I didn't see you there." She bit her lip, worried that the encounter would keep her from completing her objective. "Were you coming to visit us?"

"Only passing by." His brows drew together. "You weren't planning to go out alone, were you?"

"Aunt Eleanor is shopping this morning, and all the maids are occupied with cleaning. I plan only to walk a few blocks to call on the Duchess of Ashton, so I shall be fine—though I wish you might refrain from mentioning it to my aunt. She may not agree with my judgment."

"I rather doubt she would." He glanced up the street in the direction of Ashton House. "I will make a deal with you, Miss Irvine. I shall not mention it to your aunt if you let me remedy the situation by escorting you to see her grace."

The muscles in her midsection tightened. Subjecting herself to the duchess's mercy would be mortifying enough without another person looking on. "Thank you, Colonel, but I wouldn't want to inconvenience you. Surely I'll be safe for such a short walk."

" 'Tis no inconvenience. I've been meaning to check on her grace's health for several days." He offered his arm. "You've given me a good excuse to call."

She had no polite way to decline, so she hooked her

arm through his. They set off down St. Audley Street in silence. She refused to lose this chance to repair her aunt's friendship. After a few seconds, she cleared her throat. "I wonder, sir, if I may be so bold as to ask you a second favor?"

"Of course—but I object to the term 'second.' You've done *me* a favor, and now I will attempt to repay you."

Despite her uneasiness, she smiled. "You cannot convince me you're in my debt."

"No?" He looked at her sideways, then cast his gaze downward in a sheepish manner that surprised her. "If I didn't have your moral support, I might be too timid to make this visit. I'd thought you might have realized that, given your situation with the duke. 'Tis *he* you are truly visiting, is it not?"

"Of course not!" Shocked by his assumption about her and Adrian, it took her a moment to realize what else he had implied. The colonel had as good as confessed to a romantic interest in the duchess! She tried not to show her astonishment. "That is, I believe I understand, but not because the duke and I . . . he and I are merely friends."

"Forgive me." He looked ahead at the footpath. "I spoke out of turn. Let's get back to your question. What is the favor you seek?"

She moistened her lips. "Well, toward the end of our visit, would you mind allowing me a few minutes alone with the duchess? I require a word with her concerning a personal matter."

The colonel stopped in his tracks. "Oh, dear, I'm intruding. Now I understand why you ventured out on your own."

"No, no. Please carry on." She tugged on his arm to urge him forward. "In a way, it may help to have you along. I, too, am somewhat nervous, you see. Perhaps your presence will lend *me* courage."

The tension in his features relaxed. "If that's true, I'll be happy to grant your favor."

They resumed walking and let the subject drop, instead striking up a conversation about the opera. Considering that Maeve had missed much of the production, she discussed the topic as intelligently as she could. Before she knew it, they had reached the front steps of Ashton House.

Gazing up at the exquisite brownstone town house, she had a sudden pang of fear that they would be refused entrance. The duchess could easily plead a sick headache again.

The butler answered their knock promptly, however, and showed them inside without hesitation. Leading them to the drawing room, he bowed. "You may wait here."

Within minutes their hostess swept into the room. Her energetic gait and flushed cheeks lent her all the appearance of perfect health. "Hello, Colonel, Miss Irvine."

The visitors jumped to their feet and greeted her. Maeve's curtsy felt clumsy, but the colonel's bow had little more finesse. He appeared genuinely unnerved. If such an agreeable fellow could fall for a woman as unpleasant as the duchess, it made one wonder if the saying *there's someone for everyone* might actually have validity.

The duchess looked back and forth between them. "Why isn't Eleanor with you? Is she unwell?"

Maeve noted the furrow of concern etched in her brow and was glad to see that the woman really cared. "Auntie is fine, your grace. She has merely gone shopping with Great Aunt Lucinda. The colonel and I came to inquire after your health."

The pink in her cheeks deepened, a show of humility that softened her features rather prettily. "Thank you. I'm much improved today. Won't you have a seat?"

They all settled into chairs, but Colonel Westfall leaned forward, studying the woman. "Finding you well is a relief, your grace. Your illness seemed to come upon you so quickly—right in the middle of the Trent ball, if I'm correct. Then you declined the museum visit I proposed and missed last night's opera. I was beginning to worry about you."

"I have secluded myself more out of precaution than necessity." She looked down at her hands, folded in her lap. "Perhaps I could have gone to the opera and returned none the worse, but I wanted to avoid the crowds."

He nodded. "A wise precaution, but I hope we can schedule our museum trip soon."

Twisting a large ruby ring on her finger, the duchess looked uncharacteristically unsure of herself. "I—I thank you, but I may need a few more days to recover. They say that antiquities tend to foster bad air."

"Perhaps we should picnic instead." The colonel stopped and cleared his throat. "Along with several friends, of course. Lady Blaine and Lord Paterson might like to go—and Miss Irvine and your son."

Her gaze swept to Maeve, her features hardening instantly. Clearly the mention of her son and Maeve in one breath annoyed the woman. She looked back to the colonel with clenched teeth. "We'll discuss it in a few days."

His cheeks darkened just perceptibly. "Of course, your grace. Forgive me for rushing you. The last thing I would want is to provoke a relapse."

"No, no." She looked away and put one hand up to her forehead. "You are kind to invite me."

Maeve eyed her with curiosity. She had never seen

the duchess so flustered. The coquette of the dinner party a few nights ago was gone, yet the woman wasn't conclusive about rejecting the colonel, either. The old harridan did have some human blood in her, it seemed.

After another quarter hour of trivial conversation—Maeve contributing little—the colonel rose. "Miss Irvine has requested that before we go I allow her a few moments in private with your grace, so I shall make my farewell now. I apologize again for dropping in unexpectedly."

After a glance of surprise at Maeve, the duchess looked back at him and said, "Nonsense, Colonel. Thank you for calling. I'll have the butler show you to the morning room to wait."

"Thank you." He bowed low over her hand, then gave Maeve a wavering smile. "Please take all the time you need, Miss Irvine."

He left the room, and the duchess turned to her with wide, bright eyes. "How came it that Colonel Westfall and you should be out making calls together?"

"The colonel was passing by Aunt Eleanor's house as I left. When I mentioned I was coming here, he offered to escort me." As she recalled his sheepishness, her lips curved upward. "He's obviously quite taken with you, ma'am."

For an instant the woman only stared at her. In the end she must have seen sincerity in Maeve's silly grin, because suddenly her cheeks dimpled, too. Looking downward, she said, "Don't be absurd, gel. Now, get on with the reason you wanted to see me."

Grin fading, Maeve rubbed her palms together to try to warm her cold fingers. There was nothing for it but to plunge into what she had to say. "Aunt Eleanor has been rather down lately. She fears there may be more to your recent absence from Society than mere illness. Her theory is that you've been avoiding her."

A moment passed in silence. Quietly, the duchess said, "I was afraid of that."

"However," Maeve forced herself to continue, "I suspect that *I'm* the one you'd prefer not to see. For my aunt's sake, you and I need to talk, your grace. Are you . . . are you angry that I've been taking up so much of the duke's time?"

Her gaze dropped to her ruby again, and she twisted the ring several times before answering. "Not precisely angry. But since you ask, I shall confess I've been uneasy."

When she failed to go on, Maeve asked, "Is there some way I might put you at ease?"

"I expect not." Drawing a deep breath, the duchess looked up at her. The shine had fled from her eyes. "Miss Irvine, you've likely heard enough from Eleanor to know that over the past few years my son has suffered greatly. Belinda's loss wounded him deeply."

A lump rose in her throat. "I've no doubt of it."

The normally self-possessed woman raised her hands to rub her temples. "I'm going to be frank with you. My fear is that if he should be subjected to another ill-fated love, he might lose all capacity to live happily."

Maeve's throat tightened further, preventing her from making any response.

The duchess rose and walked to a nearby flower arrangement, fussing with the blooms. "I'm certain you're aware that Adrian has paid you far more attention than any other woman since Belinda. On the other hand, you have lavished most of your time on Charles Leight. Whatever you think of me, Miss Irvine, my son doesn't deserve such capricious treatment."

"But, ma'am, there is nothing between me and Mr. Leight."

She whirled around, a deep furrow etched into her brow. "Was he not with you for over an hour only this morning? I drove by Eleanor's house twice, and I saw his carriage parked outside both times."

Maeve swallowed with difficulty. She wished she'd never accepted the painting commission. Aunt Eleanor had been right about secrets causing nothing but trouble. "Truly, ma'am, neither he nor I have anything but platonic feelings for one another."

"Indeed? And yet you must see each other today after speaking at the opera only last night. Before you arrived, I never knew Charles to visit Eleanor for hours on end."

She opened her mouth to protest further, but before she could think what to say, a feminine laugh rang out in the hallway. The doors leading to the drawing room burst open, and Adrian walked in with Lady Louisa on his arm.

A sick knot twisted her stomach. He'd spent time in the Postlethwaites' box last night, and today he was in Lady Louisa's company again. Obviously he had focused on the debutante as a candidate to replace little Eliza's mother.

His gaze met Maeve's, and his eyes narrowed. He gave her a curt nod, then greeted the duchess in a similar manner.

His mother smiled broadly. "Adrian—and Lady Louisa. What a lovely surprise."

"Good afternoon, your grace." The debutante curtsied, then stepped forward.

While the two women exchanged pleasantries, Maeve racked her brain for an excuse to leave. Her talk with the duchess hadn't gone well, but at least she'd let the woman know Aunt Eleanor was suffering. Now she couldn't bear to sit by and watch Lady Louisa winning favor with Adrian and his mother alike.

Standing, she cleared her throat. "If you'll excuse me, Colonel Westfall is waiting to escort me home, and I cannot keep him cooling his heels."

"Westfall is here?" Adrian asked. "Where is he?"

"In the morning room," his mother replied. "He walked Miss Irvine here but . . . er, thought we might want a moment to gossip in private."

"Well, let me fetch him." Adrian turned back toward the door. "He'll hear our voices and think we've forgotten him."

Before Maeve could offer to go instead, he had bolted into the hall. Once he'd disappeared, she continued staring for another minute. Now she would be stuck here for at least a quarter hour, while Westfall made small talk with the newcomers.

Sinking back into her chair, she looked over at Lady Louisa, who was telling her hostess about the opera. The girl's eyes were bright with the spark of youth, and her fair complexion was almost luminous.

*I cannot compete with the like of her,* she thought. *I have lost that sort of glow and enthusiasm forever.*

She shifted in her seat, anxious to leave the house. Once she did, she would do her best to avoid running into Adrian again anytime soon. The best thing for her would be to sidestep him until she could get past this stupid infatuation with him.

Before going to the morning room, Adrian paused in the hallway, taking a few moments to try to compose himself. He had known that Maeve planned to call on his mother, but he had hoped she would have come and gone by the time he got home. He had purposely dallied at his banker's, then taken a long ride in Hyde Park, which was where he'd run into the Postlethwaites. The conniving Lady Postlethwaite had somehow foisted her daughter upon him, urging him to take Lady Louisa to visit his mother while she ran some other "important" errand.

Now he was somewhat glad the girl had been on his arm when he'd walked into the house. Perhaps escorting another attractive woman made him look less a fool for Maeve Irvine, who evidently juggled men as easily as her late cousin had. He, too, had driven past South Audley Street several times and noted Charles' lingering there. It was a wonder Maeve wasn't still with him. Perhaps she had cut his visit short in order to come here.

*Hmm.* He rubbed his chin. If she'd deserted a suitor in favor of pleading with his mother on her aunt's behalf, she obviously cared about Lady Blaine. Just when he had her figured for a complete witch, she had to toss in a kind gesture. Resisting her beauty would be much easier if she didn't show such signs of selflessness.

He went to the colonel and greeted the man with some reserve. Though the fellow seemed like a decent sort, Adrian didn't know what his intentions toward the duchess were. The colonel shook his hand with a little extra vigor, then looked down as if embarrassed. Adrian wasn't sure if that were a good sign or not.

When they returned to the drawing room, however, his thoughts flew back to Maeve. He noticed that while the others chatted, she sat in silence, frequently casting her gaze into her lap. Clearly she wasn't in attendance for her own enjoyment, only for her aunt's benefit.

He softened toward her. She likely wasn't even after Lady Blaine's money, especially since she had multiple men who would gladly furnish her with wealth if only she would choose one.

*But she claims she doesn't want to marry,* he remembered. Maybe she didn't want to choose one man but play a number of them off one another, much as Belinda had done.

If so, he would bloody well make sure he wasn't among them.

Lifting his chin, he stepped up to the rest of the party. As soon as there was a break in conversation, he asked his mother, "What were you and Miss Irvine discussing before Lady Louisa and I interrupted?"

She hesitated, glancing at Maeve then looking back to him. "Well, I suppose it's no secret. It shows what a thoughtless friend I am, however. Miss Irvine was kind enough to relay that Eleanor has missed hearing from me. I fear I haven't even written her a note in days. I've been rather too indulgent of my headaches. How am I to recover completely if I lounge about the house behaving like an invalid?"

"I'm a great believer in getting outdoors to exercise," the colonel said. "Don't forget that my picnic invitation still stands . . . for everyone here, of course."

"Picnic?" Lady Louisa beamed. "I love picnics."

The duchess looked at her and raised an eyebrow. "Do you, my dear?"

"Oh, yes." She turned to Westfall. "What did you have in mind, Colonel? Perhaps a jaunt upriver into the country?"

He smiled. "A lovely idea—and I think I know just the spot."

"Indeed?" The duchess smiled. "I believe you two have convinced me. Why don't we make plans for, say, Friday afternoon? I know Adrian and I have no other engagements then. Lady Louisa, will that suit you?"

"Yes, I'm free, too. Naturally, I shall have to confirm the idea with Mama, but I'm sure she'll allow me go, if you are to attend, your grace."

"Tell your mother I'd be happy to chaperon you."

Adrian simmered while his mother persisted fawning on her favorite. Kind of the duchess to answer for his availability. Now he was left either to concede or to look like a spoilsport by reneging. Hadn't he spent enough time in Lady Louisa's company lately? He had nothing against the chit, but he didn't want to give the impression he was interested in her. The only reason for him to participate was for the chance to observe his mother and the colonel, and that more out of curiosity than concern.

"Friday is perfect for me, too." The colonel looked to Maeve. "How about you and your aunt, Miss Irvine? Will you be able to make it?"

His ears perked up. Despite himself, he couldn't help thinking the picnic would be more interesting with her along.

She hesitated, noticeably avoiding meeting anyone else's gaze. "Well, I know Aunt Eleanor won't want to miss it. If I learn she has a previous engagement, I'll let you know immediately, but I feel confident we will come."

He frowned. Her reluctance made it obvious that she didn't want to go and had only made the sacrifice for her aunt. Likely if she weren't forced to attend she could have gone somewhere with Charles.

To his surprise, she glanced in his direction. While the others went on to discuss what foods to take, she rose and walked over to him. "Will you be bringing Eliza to the picnic, Adrian?"

"Why, yes. I like to spend as much time with her as I can."

"I'd be happy to help look after her."

He raised his eyebrows. Interest in his daughter always warmed his heart, and this wasn't the first time Maeve had expressed hers. If not for her vow against marriage, he might even suspect she was eager to have her own children.

"How kind of you," he said, sounding stiff to his own ears.

"Not at all. She's such a good baby. I'm also thinking that a day outdoors may provide a good opportunity for me to sketch her properly. Then I can give you that portrait I promised."

"I don't believe you promised me anything," he said, his throat tight. "But I'd love a sketch of Eliza. Thank you for offering to do one."

She shrugged. "It'll be a good way to keep myself occupied."

He frowned as she turned and walked back to her chair. She made it sound as though the outing would be barely tolerable.

Was the prospect of a picnic with him so boring that she needed to bring work to busy her mind? Would she have been so eager to sketch Eliza if Charles were among the party?

Watching her reseat herself, he crossed his arms over his chest. He supposed he should have been relieved his cousin wasn't coming so he didn't have to watch the young fop flirting with her. Instead, something nagged at him.

Perhaps he should have been more than relieved. Perhaps he should have been prepared to compete for Maeve.

Though he had doubts about her morality, he really still didn't know her well enough to judge her. Was she a practiced jade, or merely a young woman who didn't know her mind as well as she let on? If he avoided her now and someday she ended up marrying Charles, how would he feel then?

*Not very well,* a churning in his stomach told him.

He took a deep breath and strode over to stand next

to the chair where she sat. "Can I fetch you and Lady Blaine Friday—around noon perhaps?"

She looked up at him, her eyes round with surprise.

The offer had been rather abrupt, he realized with embarrassment.

His mother cleared her throat. "Adrian, Lord Paterson will no doubt be coming, too, and he lives in South Audley Street. He can collect Eleanor and Miss Irvine on his way."

"I *want* to take them, Mother," he said firmly. Instantly he realized he'd sounded rather eager.

His mother pursed her lips but said nothing more.

When he looked back at Maeve, one corner of her mouth had lifted with amusement.

"Noon will be fine. Thank you." She rose and turned to the colonel. "Are you ready to leave, sir?"

"Oh, of course . . . if you are."

"I should go, too," Lady Louisa noted, and Adrian was obliged to assure her he would drive her home.

While members of the party said good-bye to one another, he stole a last glance at Maeve and caught her gaze before she looked away quickly. Her manner didn't appear to be that of a practiced jade—more that of a shy schoolgirl.

He wasn't sure whether she'd accepted his offer on her own accord or chiefly to annoy his mother, but he was pleased that she had. Now he could hardly wait to see what unfolded at the picnic.

Lady Louisa took his arm, and it occurred to him that his mother would be pressing the chit upon him all during the picnic. He wondered if his friend Denny might be available to help occupy her while he attempted to get better acquainted with Maeve.

# Eleven

When a personal picnic invitation arrived from the duchess that afternoon, Maeve was pleased to see her aunt's spirits soar. The only remaining worry was that the weather wouldn't cooperate with their plans. Happily, that Friday dawned clear and mild, ensuring the event would indeed take place. The duchess showed up, headache-free, and Maeve breathed a sigh of relief.

At noon she sat beside Adrian on the box of his barouche. Her would-be rival, Lady Louisa, was conveniently stowed away inside the carriage with Adrian's friend Captain McDowell. The others all rode in Lord Paterson's coach.

If Adrian's separation from the debutante wasn't enough to please Maeve, his unexpected good humor would have done the trick. Ever since offering to drive her the other day, he had been all kindness toward her. One never would have known he'd been angry with her at the opera.

All would have been perfect, if she weren't trying to banish him from her mind. Sitting beside him on such a beautiful spring day, it was too tempting to fall back into wishing he were courting her.

As they set off behind the other coach, she decided it would be best to treat him with civility but not too much warmth. Pretending to study the passing buildings along the street, she asked casually, "So, where is Colonel Westfall taking us today?"

"Lord Paterson has a modest estate just outside of town. It's only a few miles up the river, but Westfall says the atmosphere is quite bucolic."

"Indeed?" She affected an air of vague interest. "Well, it will be nice to get away from the crowds for the day."

"Oh, it should be splendid. Westfall claims the setting is perfect for picnicking. He says there's even a stone circle on the property."

"A stone circle?" She swung her head around to look at him. "Like Stonehenge?"

"Yes, but not so extensive, from what I gather."

"Fascinating." Forgetting her reserve, she shifted in her seat for an easier view of him. "I've read about Stonehenge, and I've always wanted to see it. Is it true that no one knows who built these stone circles?"

He nodded. "The local people usually have some sort of folk story to explain each one. In my experience it often involves a group of pagans being turned to stone or some such nonsense."

"I'd like to hear the story behind this one. Do you suppose Lord Paterson knows it?"

"I daresay he does. We shall have to ask him to tell us."

The prospect of something so unusual to explore helped distract her from her worries. She leaned back against the seat and closed her eyes, letting the sun warm her face. A balmy breeze blew a strand of hair across her nose, and she brushed it away. "The day is absolutely beautiful."

"And not only the day."

Caught off guard, she opened her eyes and found him gazing at her.

He grinned. "That lemon yellow dress makes you

look even more delicious than usual, Maeve. All you need is a dab of meringue for a bonnet, and Gunter's confectionery could display you in the window."

Her jaw fell open. The compliment shocked her—and made her almost dizzy with excitement. Determined not to betray her feelings, she focused on a large church across the street. "You're rather merry today. Apparently you've forgiven me for accepting that inappropriate invitation from your cousin."

A second passed, but he answered with no hint of bitterness. "On the contrary, I'd like to beg *your* forgiveness for my surliness at the opera. The only one at fault was me—and possibly Charles, for not showing you more courtesy."

She didn't answer, though she could feel herself softening toward him.

"I hope he took you somewhere interesting," he said.

A catch in his voice made her suspect he wasn't sincere. Could Aunt Eleanor be right that he was jealous of Charles? She peered at him from the corner of her eye. "Why?"

His gaze didn't stray from the road. "You deserve to be entertained properly."

She frowned. Surely she had imagined the hint of sarcasm in his voice. Disgusted by her wishful thinking, she said, "Then perhaps you should concern yourself with entertaining me today."

He laughed. "Very well. I'll see what I can do."

Now she feared she should have kept her mouth shut. The last thing she needed was him trying to charm her when she was doing all she could to resist him.

She crossed her arms over her chest. "At least you're not brooding today. When we went to see Elgin's Marbles, it took all day before you loosened up."

At last, he looked at her. "Well, I'm glad you preferred that to my brooding. You didn't think that I 'loosened up' a bit too much that day?"

The memory of their kiss rushed back, and heat suffused her face. She looked into her lap. How could she answer? To imply she regretted the kiss wouldn't be honest. Finally, she murmured, "Goodness, you are mischievous today."

"Yes, we shall have to see where it leads."

Forcing herself to meet his gaze, she raised her eyebrows in an attempt to remain aloof. The grin he bestowed on her was captivating. She turned away quickly before she gave in to the temptation to smile. Allowing her hopes to seep back would only lead to pain in the end. Perhaps she would have been better off if Captain McDowell weren't present, and Lady Louisa were free to dominate Adrian's attention.

As they left the city, she directed her attention to the passing scenery, commenting now and then on nature's beauty. Before long the lead coach turned down a shady side lane that took them into a handsomely landscaped park.

"I believe we've reached Lord Paterson's estate," Adrian said, guiding the horses to follow the other coach. "He will undoubtedly know of an excellent spot to have our meal."

Indeed, his lordship led them to an ideal little grove, well secluded by picturesque clusters of trees and bushes. When Adrian stopped the barouche, Maeve jumped to the ground without waiting for his assistance. She grabbed her sketchbook and pencils from under her seat and started toward the area where the first carriage had parked. With any luck, she would not be alone with the duke again, except perhaps on the ride home.

The chirping of birds and the gurgle of a nearby stream lent tranquillity to the setting. Trying not to let her nerves spoil her enjoyment of the outing, Maeve paused to breathe in the sweet smell of honeysuckle.

She noticed her aunt spreading a gingham cloth on the grass and stooped to help. Straightening the fabric, she set down her things on one corner. "Is there anything else I can do?"

"No, thank you, dear." The countess laid a rock on the corner nearest her. "The coachman is going to lay out cushions for us to sit on, and two footmen will be arriving with food shortly."

As they stood, Lord Paterson joined them. "While we're waiting, I thought we'd walk down to the stone circle."

Aunt Eleanor smiled at him. "That sounds lovely."

The duchess approached, carrying Eliza. "I'll stay here with the baby."

"A wise choice, given that you're still recovering from your illness," Colonel Westfall said. "I'll keep you company. I've seen the stones before."

Suddenly Adrian was at Maeve's side, offering her his arm. He smiled at her, then glanced around at the others. "I was telling Miss Irvine about the stones during our drive, and she's quite eager to see them."

Seeing no other choice, she took his arm and murmured, "Thank you."

Captain McDowell paired up with Lady Louisa, and the party of six set off along the stream. Adrian adopted a slow pace, and he and Maeve began to fall to the back of the group.

Anxious to avoid being alone with him, she tried to pull him forward but succeeded only in drawing him closer to her. Luckily, before they dropped too far behind the others, the stone circle appeared in a clearing ahead.

Judging by what she had heard of Stonehenge, these

monoliths stood smaller, but the big ones still towered several feet taller than an average man. With their age estimated at thousands of years, their standing at all was a wonder. As she neared them, she imagined mysterious peoples of the past—perhaps some of them her own ancestors—dragging the heavy stones into the meticulous formation, then worshipping around them on sticky midsummer nights and crisp winter solstices.

Growing excited, she quickened her pace, dragging her escort along. "Lord Paterson, is there a local story to explain this formation?"

"As a matter of fact, 'tis the subject of much folklore." He stopped and waited for her and Adrian to catch up, then proceeded more slowly. "The locals call it the Five Witches or Five Wise Women. They say the large standing stones were formed when a group of druid priestesses who refused to accept Christianity were petrified at God's hand. The smaller ones are said to be the witches' familiars—black cats, I suppose."

Lady Louisa broke free of the captain and dashed up to a toppled stone. Climbing upon it, she surveyed her surroundings. "What a dreadful start for such a wonderful place."

Maeve took the cue to separate from the duke, as well. She strode to one of the stones and ran a hand over the surface. "I'm sure this site must once have been considered sacred. What a pity that it has since been maligned."

"I refuse to believe the witch story." Lady Louisa spread her arms wide and walked the length of her stone.

The captain stepped up and held up a hand to aid her. "'Tis nothing but nonsense."

Lord Paterson drew the countess into the center of the circle. "In some ways, many people still consider the site sacred. To this day, stories abound about performing rituals here to procure various types of good fortune."

Looking around the circle, Maeve noticed an enormous rock with a person-sized hole in the middle. She hurried toward it with Adrian trailing her. "Look at this one. I could pass right through the center!"

"That stone has a very particular superstition attached to it," Lord Paterson said.

She climbed into the formation and crouched inside, looking out into the adjacent woods.

Adrian moved around to the outside of the ring and smiled up at her, holding out his hands. "Let me help you down."

As he took her waist and eased her to the ground, Lord Paterson called from behind, "It's used for fertility rites. Women who want to have children pass through the stone into the arms of their mates."

Her gaze caught Adrian's, and he gave her a crooked grin. Embarrassed, she looked down. His hands seemed to linger at her hips for a extra second before sliding away.

"Thank you," she breathed.

"Glad to be of service."

Without looking him in the eye again, she ducked back into the circle. Everyone seemed to be smiling at her.

A nervous giggle welled up inside her and bubbled over. "In the future I shall have to be more careful about what sort of rites I accidentally perform."

They all laughed, and Lord Paterson said, "Don't worry. According to legend, the ritual is not complete without a kiss."

Taking her arm again, Adrian leaned close to her and

said below his breath, "I daresay it takes more than a kiss for that ritual to work."

She would have giggled again if she hadn't clapped a hand over her mouth. By rights, she should have been offended, but his good mood was beginning to infect her. Whenever he lavished attention upon her, she couldn't seem to help but feel happy. As they wandered out of the circle again, she tried to affect a haughty air, whispering, "There is no occasion for you to point out such a thing to me."

"There is if I want to kiss you," he said. For a moment a huge stone hid them from view of the others. He cupped her cheek and grazed her lips with his. The next instant he pulled back alongside her as they passed into view again.

She blinked in astonishment and put her fingers up to her mouth, still tingling from the contact.

Aunt Eleanor led her escort toward them. "Are you two ready to start back? I don't want to keep Jane and the colonel waiting too long."

Lord Paterson nodded. "There will be time to return here later if anyone desires."

Adrian turned to Maeve. "You and I should come back at dusk. This site must be especially magic bathed in twilight."

Struggling to recover her composure, she lifted an eyebrow. "I'm rather wary of what may lie in wait here in the dark. Besides, I want to take my time sketching Eliza."

He grinned. "As you wish."

During the walk back to the picnic area, she remained silent. To say she was confused about the resumption of his flirtation would be an understatement. How had she returned to his good graces? She almost wished his anger had lingered so she would have had more time to look at the situation with a rational eye. As it was, she felt light-headed with desire for him. The mere warmth of his arm against hers intoxicated her.

When they sat down to eat, he took the place beside her. All through the meal, she struggled to keep her composure. In his company, she felt elated, yet terrified by the feeling. Making conversation proved nearly impossible. Her aunt, however, was talking a mile a minute, clearly in the highest of spirits. Maeve concentrated on following her words and made a great effort to add an occasional comment.

After the meal, Captain McDowell and Lady Louisa rose for another walk. Adrian again invited Maeve for a short stroll.

"Thank you, but I'd like to start sketching Eliza before she grows too tired and decides to nap." She reached to the corner of the tablecloth, where she had stowed her sketchbook earlier. "I hope I can get her to sit still."

"I'll keep her occupied while you draw." He rose and picked up the baby. "Where shall we sit? Would you like to look for a scenic spot along the stream? We can take some of these cushions with us."

"No, no. There's plenty of scenery here." Maeve scanned the area and pointed to a huge oak some twenty yards away. "That tree will make a nice backdrop. Let's sit there."

He shrugged. "Whatever pleases you."

Between them they carried the baby, cushions, and drawing materials to the tree and set up facing one another. Likely tiring already, Eliza was quiet. Adrian had grabbed a picture book to read to her, and she sat more still than Maeve would have dared wish. Best of all, he was able to keep the baby laughing. Without making a conscious decision, Maeve began sketching both father and daughter, smiling to herself as she watched their playful interaction.

The work took over her mind, and time flew as the charcoal marks on her paper came to life. Eventually, the baby fell asleep, but by then Maeve was adding the final touches.

"I fear your model has quit for the day." Adrian lay the baby down on one of the cushions. Eliza didn't even stir. "May I see how far you got?"

"Yes, I'm just finishing up." Looking over the drawing, she felt her throat tighten. What a beautiful sight a father and daughter made. All she had done was copy what she had observed, and somehow the connection between the pair radiated. One could see their love in the way they looked at one another and in the cozy postures of their bodies.

"Good lord." Staring at the portrait, Adrian squatted beside her.

She smiled at him. "Do you like it?"

"I'm speechless. It's marvelous."

Her pleasure overflowed in a laugh. "You and Eliza proved excellent subjects. You have such a way with her, Adrian. What I wouldn't give to have that sort of rapport with a daughter . . ."

He looked her sharply in the eye. "But you said you don't intend to marry."

Her smile waned. She regretted her slip of tongue, yet she couldn't seem to look away from him to veil her emotions. The intimacy of the moment primed a longing in her for more. She wanted to be part of the love that had just flowed through her from her models onto the paper in her sketchbook. Her throat constricted. "You said the same thing."

They stared at each other, and her heart pounded in her chest. She could scarcely credit that they had broached the subject. Would he tell her he'd changed his mind? Would ask her to marry him now?

All at once, she knew she would say yes. She could no longer fool herself into thinking she might resist him.

Then he broke their shared stare and looked back at her drawing. "Do we know each other well enough that I can see the rest of your sketchbook now?"

A flash of disappointment quickly gave way to a sense of chagrin. She had reached the point where she wanted to open up to him. The time was perfect to share some of the private pain her sketches would reveal, but the book also contained several studies for the portrait of Charles Leight. That secret wasn't hers to share—not until after a ball the following night, where Mr. Leight would announce his betrothal.

"Soon." She picked up the book and closed it, gathering it against her body.

A crease etched his brow. "Surely you have no reason to be shy about your work at this point. So far every example I've seen has been extraordinary."

"Some of the work is personal."

"Are we not practically family?" He hesitated, then added quietly, "Maeve, I want to know you better."

Her gaze locked with his again. She considered whether Mr. Leight might be willing to overlook her sharing his secret with his cousin, but the two clearly didn't have a good relationship. To deny Adrian was painful, but she had no choice. "I want to know you, too, but there's a . . . a secret involved. Give me another few days, and it will no longer matter."

Another pause ensued. Then he looked away. "If that's how you feel, I can't very well insist upon it. I had believed you and I were growing closer."

"We are," she said.

He stood and looked off toward the picnic area. "Denny and Lady Louisa are back, and the others are packing up. Are you ready to leave?"

A flood of regret engulfed her. Damn her stupid agreement with Mr. Leight. If anyone ever offered her a secret commission again, she would refuse it. Reluctantly, she nodded.

He held out his hand and she took it, savoring the warmth of his fingers against hers. As he pulled her to her feet, she closed her eyes and let herself revel in his strength. He made her feel small and protected, almost like a child again. Under his touch, her body relaxed.

Suddenly the sketchbook slipped from her grasp.

It fell to the ground, opening to a study of Charles Leight. She made a swipe to grab it but only managed to flip several pages over. Fervently, she hoped that Adrian hadn't had time to recognize his cousin—but the new page was almost as mortifying. The sketch depicted a nude male study that she had copied from a book about Greek statues. With her usual care for detail, she had breathed more life into her rendition than the original plate possessed.

She scooped up the book and clapped it shut, but she knew she hadn't been quick enough. Before she even looked up at Adrian, she felt his cold stare. When she met his gaze, she willed herself not to blush. Really, he had no right to take offense at the nude. As a serious student of art, she had perfectly good reason to study the human body.

A quavering giggle escaped her. In a desperate attempt to make light of the situation, she said, "One of my favorite models."

His face only grew stonier.

"So it would appear," he said finally.

He bent and picked up Eliza. Draping the baby against his chest, he walked off toward the picnic area.

"Oh, Adrian, don't be a prude," she called, starting after him. "Why should that drawing surprise you? You know me well enough that you should expect my sketchbook to be a little daring."

He didn't even stop or turn around, let alone answer her.

She quickened her pace, moving alongside him. "Who are you to judge, anyway? Why, you're the one who took me to see Elgin's Marbles in all of their glorious nudity."

He let out a snort, glancing over at her. "This is rather different, don't you think?"

"How so?" She threw her hands up in exasperation. "I suppose you assume the Parthenon artist was male. Perhaps our society deems the nude body beyond the pale for a young female's eyes, but you know how serious I am about my art. Do you truly expect me to pass up a chance to depict such beauty?"

"Oh, no. That would be too much to ask." He put his free hand up to his temples and squeezed. "Frankly, Maeve, I don't want to discuss it."

He strode on, and as they were nearing the rest of the party, she gave up on the conversation. Stopping, she turned around and went back to gather up her things. Her time in his good graces certainly hadn't lasted long. If he had actually cared about her, he would have wanted her to pursue her art to the fullest.

As she stacked up the cushions and placed her sketchbook on top, her body felt heavy and hard to move. She had to acknowledge the truth: She was in love with a man who didn't respect her work.

Her lower lip quivered, and she bit it in anger at her weakness, as well as his stupidity. How hypocritical of him to stare in awe at her drawings one minute, then turn up his nose the next. Surely she didn't want to marry such a man.

But the next time he began flirting with her, would she be able to keep her resolve?

She dragged her feet back to the rest of the party. As they prepared to leave, she claimed she was too cold to sit on the box with Adrian again. Instead, she rode inside with Lady Louisa and the captain until they got out at their respective houses. For the short remainder of the ride, she felt more alone than she had since moving to England.

When they pulled up in front of her aunt's house, Lord Paterson's carriage had not yet arrived. She didn't think to jump out of the barouche quickly, so she had to concede to letting Adrian open the door for her.

Climbing out, she refused to meet his gaze. "Thank you."

He gave her a stiff bow and walked her the few yards to the front steps. "Shall I wait inside with you until Lady Blaine arrives?"

"No, don't concern yourself with me," she said, imitating his chilly air. She gave him one last glance as she opened the door. "Just turn me over to the Greeks, Troilus."

Stepping inside, she shut the door in his face.

Inside the house, she felt a rush of satisfaction. For once she had stood up for herself, even if her words might have been a little obscure. Like Troilus with Cressida, Adrian fawned on her for a brief period, then dropped her at the first sign of difficulty. She thought he would understand her reference. They had discussed the play on several occasions.

Lifting her chin, she walked to staircase and began to ascend. About halfway up, she suddenly realized she was empty-handed. She'd left her sketchbook in Adrian's barouche.

*Blast it!*

She spun around and ran back down the stairs. Flinging open the front door, she burst out onto the step. He was gone. She looked up the street, then down to the other end. There was no sign of his barouche.

Her shoulders slumped. She leaned back against the doorjamb, defeated. After all she had been through to protect Mr. Leight's secret, it would be exposed now, at the last minute.

Or would it? Perhaps Adrian wasn't likely to look inside the carriage before tomorrow night, when Mr. Leight intended to present the portrait. He normally rode outside. She could call at Ashton House the next day and retrieve it.

Her body tensed. She wasn't ready to face him again. Perhaps she could put off the visit, and he wouldn't see the book—or wouldn't look through it if he did.

Running her fingers through her hair, she straightened up and turned back into the house. She would calm herself down, then decide what to do. Right now she was just too overwhelmed.

# Twelve

Adrian drove his horses through the London streets at a thundering clip. Maeve's curt dismissal of him had stoked the wrath he'd been suppressing since he'd glimpsed Charles's image among her drawings. He still couldn't believe she had *laughed* when her sketchbook fell open to that shameless nude portrayal. *A favorite model,* she had said. It had been shocking enough to find his cousin's face in her sketchbook, let alone all of him.

He clenched his teeth, recalling how the peacock had posed without an ounce of reserve—and how she had depicted every last detail of his form. The intimacy of such a sitting left no reasonable doubt that they were lovers. She hadn't even shown any shame about being exposed. If anything, she'd behaved as though *she* had reason to be vexed.

*The nerve she had slamming the door in my face,* he thought. And what in blazes had she meant by comparing him to Troilus? How was he leaving her to the Greeks? Was she suggesting that he had led her into Charles's arms? Was there something about him that drove the women he wanted to other men?

Barreling around a corner, he nearly grazed a passing produce wagon. He took a deep breath and slowed the horses, telling himself his thoughts had taken an irrational turn. For safety's sake, he struggled to blot out his anger. Why did he care about that little jade, anyway? She was obviously no better than Belinda—maybe worse. Maeve couldn't even seem to *pretend* she fit in with respectable society. Poor Lady Blaine was in for a shock when she realized what a disgraceful life her niece really led.

Blast it, he would likely have to warn the countess himself, he realized. He couldn't allow Maeve to continue as she was and risk her tainting her aunt's reputation. Lady Blaine was Eliza's grandmother, for goodness sake.

He steered into Grosvenor Square, where the unwelcome sight of Lord Paterson's carriage met him in front of his house. Apparently he and the colonel were still with this mother.

Driving past without stopping, he headed for his club. White's had lost much of its charm for him years ago, but in such a mood, the distractions of alcohol and gaming still beckoned.

While he tossed back drinks with a horde of gamesters, he never stopped thinking about Maeve. She had allowed him to kiss her, even though she was already involved with Charles. Well, she'd always claimed she didn't want to marry, so he supposed she felt no need to limit herself to one man.

Was it only carte blanche she'd been looking for, then? Would she have chosen him over Charles as a protector if he'd pursued her more aggressively? Taking on a mistress who was living with his mother-in-law wasn't quite ideal, but, frankly, if Maeve were going to be sleeping with someone, it might as well be him. Perhaps he could set her up in her own house. . . .

*Oh, hell.* He held his head, which had started to ache. Such thoughts about his late wife's cousin were disgraceful. His desire for her had truly driven him to distraction.

After he'd passed more hours at White's than he cared to count, the sharpness of his anger had dulled, usurped by numb misery. A sluggish ride in the crisp night air brought him home again, where he found minor cause for comfort: The house stood dark. He wouldn't have to face his mother.

Pulling the barouche around back, he tossed the reins to a stable hand and got out, heading toward the door to the kitchen.

"Your grace?" the boy called after him.

Adrian stopped without turning, one hand on his brow. "What is it?"

"You left something in the gig."

He looked around and saw the lad holding up a large black volume—Maeve's sketchbook. A wave of nausea swelled inside of him. The damned thing had followed him home.

The stable hand frowned and looked more closely at his find. "Don't you want it?"

"Not in the least." He started to walk away again, but a vision of all the servants in his household snickering over Maeve's drawings made him stop. He spun around and retraced his steps. "On second thought, I had best take it."

"Yes, your grace." The boy had already put the book back, but he pulled it out again and handed it over.

Adrian took the volume and stalked into the house, holding it by one corner as though it dripped mud. Upon reaching his study, he threw it onto the desk and reached for a decanter of brandy. When he pulled out the stopper, however, the sticky smell of the alcohol made him feel sick. He closed the bottle again and set it down. He'd had enough to drink.

He'd had enough of everything.

Dragging himself across the room, he flopped down on a stiff-backed couch. The cushions were hard, and his clothes dug into his neck and waist. He knew he should go to bed, but the room had begun to spin. Exhausted both physically and emotionally, he could no longer will himself to move. He loosened his cravat and let his body slump.

Eventually, exhaustion obscured everything else, and he dropped off to sleep.

"Adrian? Adrian?"

The duchess's voice tore through the veil of slumber, searing Adrian's eardrums. He squinted against the sunlight streaming in through a window. "Mother?"

"Why on earth are you sleeping in the study?"

The study? He rubbed his eyes and looked around the room, spotting Maeve's sketchbook on the desk. The memory of the whole miserable night flooded back. "Oh, hell."

"For all I knew, you never even came home last night." The duchess marched up to stand in front of him, putting her hands on her hips. "I was worried sick about you until Bernard told me he'd seen you in here this morning."

He focused on her, surprised to find that somehow she looked more vibrant than she had in years. The crisp green cambric she wore emphasized the color of her eyes and set off her auburn hair. In contrast he felt like a derelict.

"Must I account for every move I make?" he muttered.

"No, but this behavior isn't like you. You're past the age of carousing all night."

"I should also be past the age of being scolded by my mother, but that never seems to deter you." He ran a hand through his hair to try to smooth it down. "Why did you want me, anyway? I need to go upstairs and pull myself together."

"Indeed. You look a sight. Do you know what time it is?" She glanced at a grandfather clock in the corner of the room. "Nearly two in the afternoon. 'Tis fortunate that men don't require as meticulous a toilette as women. We have a ball to attend tonight."

He snorted. "I won't be attending any balls tonight—or perhaps for a long time."

"You'd better attend this one." She moved to a side table that held a pitcher and glasses and filled one of the tumblers with water. Walking back to him with the drink, she said, "Charles sent a note around this morning urging us to go. I don't know why it's so important to him, but he begs us to be there as a personal favor."

*Charles.* The last person on earth he wanted to see.

"Why should we consider any favor that coxcomb asks for?" He took the glass and stared into the water, trying to work up the will to swallow anything. "He has always thrown any attempt we made to help him back in our faces."

"He is still family. If he's in some sort of trouble, we must at least discover what the matter is. If it comes down to upholding the family name and honor, we have no choice but to help him."

A sickening possibility occurred to him. What if Charles had gotten Maeve with child? But surely even that idiot wouldn't choose to discuss such a matter at a ball. "If he has a problem, why wouldn't he call on us here?"

"I don't know. Perhaps he has no problem. His note says nothing more than what I've told you."

Adrian forced down a gulp of water. He had half a mind to go and put his fist through his cousin's face for abusing Lady Blaine by sleeping with her houseguest. For form's sake, he supposed he couldn't create such a scene at a ball, but he would certainly waste no time in speaking to Charles. He'd warn him to redirect his sexual exploits away from the family's doorstep or else. The fact that he, too, still wanted Maeve was another matter—one he would have to resolve later.

"Very well, I'll go," he said. "I need to talk with Charles anyway. I may as well do it at a bloody ball."

"Adrian! I'll not countenance my son using such coarse language." She headed toward the door to the hallway. "I expect you to turn around your mood by eight tonight."

He didn't answer. If his mood had changed at all by then, it would likely only be worse.

At the threshold, his mother paused and glanced back over her shoulder. "Oh, I nearly forgot. Miss Irvine called for you earlier."

His gaze shot to meet hers. "Maeve was here?"

She lifted one eyebrow.

Immediately he was sorry that he'd revealed any interest. He looked down into his glass, his mind racing. Had she come to try to explain her indiscretion with Charles? To confess that she actually would prefer him to his cousin as a lover? Of course she'd probably only come to fetch her sketchbook. "Did she say what she wanted?"

"No, and she didn't ask to see me when Bernard told her that you weren't home. Her manners are rather . . . foreign, to put it mildly. 'Tis not at all proper for an unmarried woman to visit a bachelor."

He rolled his eyes. "I *am* her cousin by marriage."

Why he was defending the chit he didn't know—habit, he supposed.

"In any case, there's no need for you to return her call. You'll doubtlessly see her at the Baylors' ball tonight. Eleanor told me they plan to attend."

As she left the room, he flopped back on the couch. *Brilliant.* Another opportunity to view her and Charles doting upon each other—unless *somehow* he could steal her away for himself.

He clenched his jaw. For the first time he realized how much he wanted her, even as a mistress if he couldn't have her for a wife. Obviously she wasn't indifferent to him, and he felt more for her than he was willing to contemplate. In many ways she was different from any other woman he knew. She had a forthright air about her quite the opposite of that of many British females. And for all that her relationship with Charles riled him, he couldn't accuse her of deceiving him. Though he had kissed her, he had given her no hint as to his intentions.

A stab of guilt cut through him. What if, in fact, she had maintained her virtue until his ambiguity drove her to Charles? He knew his cousin to be practiced in the art of seduction. If Maeve had fallen prey to him, she lacked moral fortitude, but Adrian wasn't blameless either. He hadn't acted honorably toward her. An honorable man didn't kiss a well-bred woman without a declaration.

Was that why she had called him Troilus? When he'd given her no indication of his intentions, perhaps she had turned to his cousin instead. Perhaps she actually returned the feelings he had for her but didn't believe *he* was serious.

The least he could do was offer her his protection. It would be no favor—he wanted her for his—but he could afford to support her in a style Charles couldn't match. And he didn't see himself ever tiring of her. He felt he could promise her a degree of security.

He hoisted himself to his feet. Could he really betray his mother-in-law like this? If Lady Blaine ever learned that her niece had become his mistress, she would no doubt cut off all relations with him. And what would happen to her relationship with Eliza?

A wave of dizziness came over him. Perhaps it made more sense to try to convince Maeve to marry him—but would she agree to remain constant, and, if so, could he believe her?

Before he made any decision, he needed to talk to her and determine how much she felt for him . . . and how much for Charles.

He grabbed her sketchbook and took it up to his bedchamber, not daring to let the book out of his sight. Ordering a hot bath, he tried to clear his mind and focus on the points he needed to communicate to her that evening—and the details he needed to ascertain.

Maeve huddled under an umbrella with her aunt, standing in a light rain outside of Baylor House. Some twenty guests waited ahead of them in line to be received.

She shivered and pulled her useless lace shawl more tightly around her. What a wretched night for a ball. She had no wish to make small talk and pretend to be interested in young fops who asked her to dance or old harpies who quizzed her for gossip. The fact that Charles would be presenting her painting hardly made up for such annoyances. She was relieved that the secret would soon be out but too dejected about Adrian's treatment of her to feel any real pleasure.

"Here are Jane and Adrian." Aunt Eleanor poked her head from under the umbrella and waved toward a carriage that had just pulled up.

*Perfect,* Maeve thought. *Shall I expect to be upbraided, or has he had time to revert to a flirtatious mood?*

She stole a peek as he emerged from the carriage and held the door for his mother. Impeccably clad in formal black, he looked more handsome than ever. From his posture alone, she could tell that he wasn't brooding, so perhaps he would try to flirt. Sighing, she let her gaze slide from the perfectly fitted broad shoulders of his jacket past his slim waist and muscular thighs to the tips of his gleaming Hessian boots.

He turned around and caught her staring.

She looked away, feigning an interest in passing traffic. Though she didn't turn back, she could feel him approaching. *Make no allowances for him,* she warned herself. His playful moods never lasted long, and in the end he always seemed to find some reason to disapprove of her.

"Hello, Lady Blaine, Miss Irvine." He bowed to them as he and the duchess joined them.

She nodded and let her aunt greet the newcomers with more enthusiasm. Fortunately the countess was more excited about the ball than she. The woman talked nonstop for the next five minutes. Maeve comprehended nothing of what she said.

As the line before them waned and they neared the front steps, Adrian took her by the elbow. "Mind the puddle, love."

She started and barely managed not to tread in the water. He had called her *love.* True, the endearment could be heard a dozen times a day on any English street, but *he* had never called *her* "love" before.

Now was not a good time for him to start.

Stepping over the puddle, she smirked at him. "What, no offer to throw down your jacket for me to walk upon?"

He shrugged. "I suspect an independent woman such as you would only find Sir Walter Raleigh's style pretentious. Now, I wonder how an ancient Greek courtier might attend his lady on a rainy evening. Would he throw his toga down for her? Or must he wait until the wedding night for that?"

Her jaw dropped. He had no place using such warm speech with her, especially when he always judged *her* peccadillos so harshly.

She yanked her arm from his grasp and turned her back on him. What on earth had come over him? Perhaps second thoughts over his last attack on her had somehow sparked this behavior. Perhaps he was trying to prove he could be as impetuous as the next fellow.

Well, she had seen the reverse side of his personality far too often to be impressed.

"How unfortunate this weather is," he said softly, close to her ear. "I had hoped you would join me on the terrace tonight, as you did at the last ball we attended. Do you suppose this drizzle might let up long enough for us to steal a few moments outside?"

She snorted. "The terrace will hold no allure for me this evening, I assure you."

"Hmm. Finding a spot away from the crowd is more difficult when one is limited to the inside of the house."

"Then I suppose you will have to face the crowd." She reached into her reticule, affecting to search for something. "One does have to tolerate society occasionally, you know."

He paused, then spoke in a more sober tone. "You're clearly vexed with me, and I believe I have an idea why.

In order to try to make things up to you, I really need a word alone with you. Perhaps we can take a stroll through the portrait gallery sometime tonight. The word is that Mr. Baylor has a good art collection."

The romantic scene he suggested flashed in her mind before she could suppress her imagination. The gallery, dimly lit by candles, would stretch before the two of them, a spacious relief from the stifling ballroom. He would hold her hand, and she would revel in the secure warmth of his fingers.

"Will you join in me in the gallery, then?" he asked.

She met his gaze, warm and inviting, and actually had to fight off the urge to accept him. Outrageous! She looked back down to her reticule. "Thank you, but I . . . I don't know. We shall have to see if we have time."

Making a show of pulling out a handkerchief and dabbing at her nose, she glanced at her aunt and the duchess. The two older women remained deep in conversation.

"Colonel Westfall says . . ." drifted over the other chatter in the foyer, then got lost among the noise.

Maeve knew the subject would hold both ladies rapt for a long time. She shoved the handkerchief back in her bag and muttered, "Sometimes I wish my aunt were a sharper chaperon."

After her remark, Adrian grew quiet.

By the time they approached their hosts in the receiving line, she was able to conduct herself with more aplomb. Curious about Mr. Leight's fiancée, she held Pamela Baylor's gaze longer than that of the young woman's parents. A tall redhead, Miss Baylor had fine features but a haughty air. Aunt Eleanor had told Maeve that the debutante had a considerable dowry—nice for Mr. Leight, whose expectations were questionable.

Maeve shook her hand. "Your ball is a huge success,

Miss Baylor. 'Tis the biggest crowd I've seen since arriving in England."

"Thank you for coming," the young woman said without smiling. In fact, her green eyes appeared to narrow, as though she were studying her guest.

Somewhat unnerved, Maeve bobbed a curtsy. "Thank you for inviting my aunt and me."

The reminder of her aunt prompted her to look around for the countess as she and Adrian moved past their hosts. She couldn't see Aunt Eleanor anywhere. Disoriented by the crowd, she allowed him to take her arm again while they inched through the hall.

When they reached the ballroom, the heat of thousands of candles and hundreds of bodies oppressed her. His touch provided an anchor of security within the kaleidoscopic confusion of pastel gowns, clashing perfumes, and amalgamated chatter overriding the chords of the orchestra.

He leaned close to her, so she could just hear him above the din. "If we ever reach the dance floor, perhaps we should take advantage of it immediately. If this throng grows any denser, we may not want to attempt dancing later."

"Thank you, but it's rather too hot for me already. I prefer to sit."

He opened his mouth as if to protest, then closed it and nodded. Scanning the area, he pointed across the room. "There's a free settee over near the windows."

Somewhat overwhelmed—as usual—by his attentions, she let him lead her through the crowd. They sat down, and she felt the tantalizing heat of his thigh against hers. Closing her eyes, she felt helplessly in love. *Stupid!*

She opened her eyes and looked around the room. No one else she recognized was within sight. With the highly eligible Duke of Ashton beside her, many of the other gentleman would be too intimidated to try to speak to her anyway.

"You look as though you've already had your fill of the ballroom," Adrian said. "Shall we go in search of the gallery now or endure this commotion a bit longer?"

She frowned, refusing to meet his gaze. "I'm not going to the gallery with you."

"Don't stay cross with me, Maeve." His tone softened. "Please. I need to talk to you. It's important."

At last, she looked him in the eye. She was tired of trying to fend off his charm, failing, and then being stung by him later. No matter what, she would not set herself up for another fall tonight.

Casting her gaze downward, she noticed a tiny speck of brown on the silver fabric near the hem of her dress. "Oh, dear, I seem to have splashed mud on my gown, in spite of your warning about that puddle. I'd best tend to these spots before they soak into the fabric."

She sprang to her feet before he could inspect the damage himself. When she glanced at him again, to her surprise, she found his gaze fixed on her face instead of her hem. His sad expression brought to mind the way he had looked the time he'd offered his condolences over her father's death—full of compassion.

"If you'll excuse me . . ." she croaked and darted into the thickest part of the crowd.

Without looking back to see if he followed, she pressed her way toward the main hall, the most probable location of the ladies' retiring room. How on earth would she possibly endure the rest of the evening? She only hoped that she could reach privacy without any acquaintances noticing how flustered she was.

At last she escaped the ballroom and turned down a corridor toward the back of the house. Several giggling debutantes emerged from a well-lit room, and she figured that must be her destination.

"Miss Irvine!" a man's voice called behind her.

For an instant she feared it was Adrian, but she realized it wasn't his voice—or his address.

A large warm hand landed on her shoulder. "Miss Irvine, I'm so pleased to find you."

She turned around to face Charles Leight, grinning broadly. "Oh. Hello, Mr. Leight."

He shifted to stand beside her, his hand still on her shoulder. Leaning close to her ear, he whispered, "I so look forward to presenting the portrait tonight. How can I ever thank you enough, Miss Irvine? You won't even let me pay you."

"There's no need. It was my pleasure." Despite her frayed nerves, she couldn't help but feel gratified by his excitement. "Just remember that the oils are still not quite dry. For the next several weeks you'll have to take care."

His eyes widened as if he were shocked that she imagined he might not do so. "But of course! I'll be certain to pass along the word to Pamela and her family . . . as well as the servants."

She smiled. "Well, that covers nearly everyone—though I suppose you still could publish a notice in the newspaper."

"Haha!" Obviously in the highest spirits, he put his arm around her and squeezed. "What a marvelous betrothal gift you've given us. I can't wait to see the look on Pamela's face when she views it for the first time."

Laughing, she hugged him back. "I hope the moment lives up to your expectations."

As she looked over his shoulder, she discovered they weren't alone in the hallway. Pamela Baylor stood several yards away. Her hard gaze burned into Maeve's. An instant later, the woman ducked through an archway that led into the ballroom.

"Oh, dear." Pulling away from Mr. Leight, she frowned. "Miss Baylor saw us just now. I'm afraid she witnessed our embrace. She was looking daggers at me."

"Where?" He spun around to view the now vacated spot.

"She went into the ballroom—through that first archway."

"I'd better see if I can find her." He glanced at her one last time. "Don't worry. I won't let a little misunderstanding spoil this evening."

Watching him dash after his fiancée, she bit her lip and prayed that he was right. In her experience, some unforeseen mishap always spoiled the evenings that one most hoped would turn out perfect.

Sighing, she continued down the hall and entered the ladies' room. For a quarter hour or so, she dallied inside, dabbing a handkerchief at imaginary spots on her hem. After one of the Baylors' maids had twice offered to help her, she began to feel conspicuous and left. Wondering what to do next, she wandered back into the ballroom.

The opening strains of a waltz caressed her ears. Instinctively, she glanced around the room for Adrian. She failed to locate him or anyone else she knew.

"Miss Irvine?" a voice asked from behind her.

She turned around to see a young footman attired in formal livery and a powdered wig.

"Yes?"

"Message for you, Miss." He thrust a note into her hand, then scurried away before she had a chance to make inquiries.

She looked down at the folded paper and read "Miss

M. I.," brandished across the front in an elaborate hand she did not recognize. What now? Perhaps Mr. Leight had written to tell her he had resolved matters with his fiancée. She hoped so.

Moving to an isolated corner of the room, she opened the gilded stationery to read the note:

*Dearest Miss I,*

*I understand that you take some interest in fine arts. Your host, Mr. Baylor, is somewhat renowned for his collection of paintings. The finest are displayed in the gallery, which runs along the south side of the house. Please meet me in the back hallway beyond the drawing room, and I shall be honored to escort you through the collection.*

*Your humble and obedient servant*

So Adrian rather than Mr. Leight had sent the note. The absence of a signature and the stilted tone might have thrown her, but the subject matter gave away his identity. She could only suppose he had ferreted out the gallery and sent a servant to fetch her, omitting their names in case someone intercepted the message.

Fearing that someone might yet see her reading it and grow curious, she refolded the paper and stowed it in her reticule. Meet him in the back hallway? She would do no such thing.

*Where is my aunt?* she thought with some desperation.

She looked around the room but saw only strangers—dancing, talking, and laughing. Everyone but she seemed to be having a wonderful time. No one except she stood alone.

A trickle of perspiration rolled down her right temple, and she swiped it away. Never had she felt so inelegant and unpopular.

The note in her reticule haunted her. If Mr. Baylor's collection truly were renowned, he would surely expect, even encourage, tonight's guests to seek out the paintings. Other art lovers would no doubt be milling about the gallery, making the area an acceptable retreat from the heat of the ballroom. Besides Adrian, she would likely find several other companionable people present.

Was she only rationalizing her desire to meet him in a secluded corner? Perhaps . . . but she could not find the will to stand outcast in a stifling ballroom while he cooled his heels in a well-stocked gallery.

Her mind made up, she scurried toward the south side of the house. She found the back hallway dark and empty. It appeared that Mr. Baylor's paintings were not attracting many guests after all. Two rows of uninvitingly closed doors stretched out before her. She nearly changed her mind and left until she noticed light coming from the last doorway on the right.

She started down the long hall, the muffled noises of the ballroom diminishing with each step. Soon she could hear her own satin slippers padding on the hardwood floor. The growing quiet and decreasing candlelight began to work on her nerves. What if someone other than Adrian had sent the note? New doubts about meeting the sender rose inside her.

Slowing her pace, she stopped a yard away from the doorway, prepared to turn and run if necessary. Even from this perspective, she could see a vast, heavily furnished salon beyond the doorway. Numerous large paintings lined the walls, lit by a blazing fire and a fair number of candles.

She inched closer to get a better look. The room

stood empty. Apparently, Adrian hadn't yet arrived. Rather ungentlemanly of him to keep her waiting.

As she scanned the area, a huge painting on the opposite wall grabbed her attention. Was that a Van Dyck?

Fascinated, she crossed the room.

# Thirteen

For the tenth time or more, Adrian looked up and down the main hall. The door to the ladies' retiring room opened, and another two giggling debutantes emerged. Still no sign of Maeve.

*I never should have let her out of my sight,* he thought. He'd nearly lost her once earlier, when she'd jumped up from the settee they'd shared and dashed through the ballroom. That time he had found her again moments later, speaking to Charles. If he'd had any sense, he would have interrupted them, but their cozy posture had stopped him. Instead, he had stormed off in a fit of jealousy. By the time he had returned, both of them were gone. Now he'd spent a quarter hour searching the crowd but couldn't locate either one of them.

Likely they were off together trysting. He clenched his fists at his sides. The wet weather would prevent them from wandering off in the gardens, but if two people didn't want to be found, they would find a way to hide. A house this size had plenty of secluded corners.

"Pardon me—your grace?" a feminine voice addressed him from behind.

He turned around to see a vaguely familiar young woman, no doubt someone he'd met earlier. *Ah, of course, the debutante of honor tonight.* "Yes, Miss Baylor?"

"I come on a somewhat unusual errand." She glanced downward, evidently unsure of her reception. "I hope you won't think me an alarmist, but . . . if I'm not mistaken, did you not escort Miss Irvine here tonight?"

"Yes, why?" He frowned. "Has she fallen ill? I've been looking for her, but I can't seem to locate her."

"I just saw her heading back toward my father's gallery . . . alone. I wasn't sure whether to go after her or if she might want privacy, but I must tell you: That part of the house is rather dark and secluded. I'm not certain a woman should be on her own back there."

He nodded, though privately he doubted she would be alone for long. His cousin was likely already awaiting her. "You were right to alert me, Miss Baylor. Thank you. I'll go after her directly. What is the quickest route from here?"

She gave him a smile that struck him as strangely sly. "That archway across the ballroom leads to the back corridor. Turn left and follow it to the end. You'll find the gallery on the right-hand side."

He bobbed a bow, then darted through the crowd. Whatever Maeve and Charles had done in the past, he wasn't about to let them risk scandalous behavior here at a well-attended ball. His family honor was at stake . . . and perhaps something else he didn't want to take time to examine.

For a change he wove easily through the dancing couples and gossiping matrons. He ducked into the back corridor and slipped quickly down the hall. Near the end he spotted an open door and held his breath, preparing himself for a sight he dreaded. The mere anticipation of witnessing Maeve and his cousin entangled in a passionate embrace made him feel nauseous.

When he stepped through the doorway, however, he

found only Maeve. He paused and glanced around the room to confirm her solitude, then looked back at her.

Intent on studying a large painting, she didn't even notice his arrival. She certainly didn't appear to be eagerly awaiting a lover. Was it possible she had ventured here only to view the artwork?

For a long moment, he stood staring, drinking in the way the firelight highlighted her classic profile and the soft contours of her frame. The crackling of the flames and the patter of rain on the windows provided a tranquil backdrop after the din of the ball. The gallery was like another world, one only he and Maeve occupied.

Stepping into the room, he was aware that he was also crossing some abstract threshold. The atmosphere in the room was so intimate. Could he possibly walk up to her without spilling everything he felt for her?

He wasn't sure—but he knew he didn't want to leave.

"Maeve?"

Her head jerked around, but when she saw him, her features and body relaxed. "So you have come."

The words confused him. Then he remembered that he had proposed showing her the gallery. He nearly laughed with relief. She hadn't come here to meet Charles at all. Apparently, she had half expected *him* to join her.

Grinning, he stepped up beside her. "I thought you had no intention of meeting me."

She didn't look as pleased as he felt. Unsmiling, she turned back toward the painting. "As you have so often pointed out, my sense of propriety is not the sharpest. Why should things be any different tonight?"

More perplexing words. Her tone sounded resentful . . . as well as despondent. His behavior toward her really had hurt her. He was almost positive of it.

When he didn't respond, she turned and gazed up at

him with eyes so large and full of sorrow that the urge to comfort her overpowered all of his doubts about her. He closed the remaining space between them and reached up to cup her cheek. Bending, he kissed her on the mouth.

She moaned and let her lips part. He deepened the kiss and tasted her tongue, but a sense of melancholy tempered his passion. He had her in arms, where he wanted her—but he had no right to her.

Pulling away from her lips, he touched his forehead to hers. After a moment, he straightened and met her gaze. The sadness in her eyes hadn't lessened. Clearly she had no expectations of him. She wasn't after his money or his title. He realized that she had kissed him only because she wanted *him.* Despite himself, a rush of excitement coursed through him.

He pushed a stray lock of her hair behind her ear. "Maeve, I've done you a great disservice, giving in to my desire for you without clarifying my intentions."

She stared at him, but her expression went blank.

Who could blame her if she wanted to hide her feelings? Unsure whether or not she truly preferred him to Charles, he still felt reluctant to expose his own—but he had to try.

He cleared his throat. "I never thought I'd say this, but I believe I've finally come to appreciate Cressida. Perhaps 'tis true that Troilus owed her more than he gave her. Tell me—and be candid, please—did I play a part in driving you to take Charles as a lover?"

Her jaw dropped. Instead of bursting into a tearful confession as he'd envisioned she might, she glared at him. Shrugging off his hold, she took a step backward. *"What?"*

"Maeve, darling, please don't think I mean to censure you for your indiscretions." He took a step toward her, but she backed away again and he stopped. "On the contrary, I'm only trying to tell you that I can see how some of the blame may lay with me."

She shook her head. "This is why you asked me to meet you here? You went to all the trouble of sending me a secret note so you could accuse me of being a lightskirt?"

"Secret note?" He frowned. "What note?"

"Actually, it was *I* who sent the note," a loud feminine voice interrupted from the doorway.

He looked over to see Miss Baylor leaning against the doorjamb, smirking.

"If you're going to tryst in the future, Miss Irvine, do it with your own escort. Make sure you don't step on another woman's toes—especially not mine." She straightened and grabbed the doorknob. "I only hope no one discovers you two alone in here together. Wouldn't it be a shame if Miss Irvine were compromised, and the two of you would be forced to marry?"

She flashed a key in front of her face, then slipped into the hall and shut the door.

The telltale clicking of a lock finally spurred Adrian out of his shocked immobility. He ran to the door and jiggled the knob, but the catch held fast. The door was solid oak and the brass bolt gleamed like new. "Blast it, this is an uncommonly solid lock."

He yanked and shoved several more times without the door budging. At last, he turned around. "It looks as though I'll need some sort of tool."

To his astonishment, his companion had vanished.

"Maeve?"

He scanned the room and stopped at an open window. Surely, she wouldn't venture outside in the rain.

But if crossing an ocean didn't daunt her, a few drops of rain weren't likely to slow her down. He ran to the window and stuck his head out in the drizzle. A long row of hedges ran along the side of the house with only a narrow stretch behind it. Maeve would have ruined her dress squeezing behind the greenery, and he would be hard pressed to move in the space at all, but he had to follow her and ensure that no harm came to her.

He climbed over the sill and looked up and down the outside wall, raindrops splattering on his face. To his left, he heard faint music coming from the ballroom. To the right, all was quiet. Which direction would she have taken?

His best guess was that she wouldn't reenter the ball in a soaked gown. He set off in the opposite direction.

Maeve stood on the terrace outside the ballroom, brushing bits of shrubbery off her shoulders. Squinting at her reflection in the window of a French door, she tried to smooth down her hair. Returning to the ball in such a state might ruin her as thoroughly as being found in the gallery with Adrian, but dallying out here in the rain would only serve to get her wetter.

She tried the doorknob and was relieved when it turned. Slipping into the house, she glanced around the surrounding area. The flirting couples and jabbering matrons in her vicinity took no note of her.

Ducking behind an ornamental screen, she scurried toward the archway that led to the back corridor. She made it without being waylaid. From there, she had no trouble reaching the ladies' retiring room.

The same servant who had earlier offered her help looked her over with an expression of dismay. "Oh, Miss, what ever has happened to you? Let me fetch you a towel."

Fortunately, only two other guests were in the room,

and as one was crying and the other comforting her, they paid no heed to Maeve's arrival.

"I . . . er, started to feel faint and stepped outside for some air," Maeve told the maid as the girl dabbed at her skirt. "Then I found I'd locked myself out. I had to locate another door before I could get back inside."

"You poor creature." The servant moved around to her back. "Happily, your dress isn't too bad off—only a little damp. No one will even notice, especially with the way some ladies are known to dampen their clothes purposely these days in order to get their skirts to cling."

Maeve frowned, glancing across the room into a cheval mirror. She didn't look as bedraggled as she expected, and if she were taken for the sort of woman who resorted to dampening her clothing, she supposed it didn't make much difference. *Some* people already seemed to think her a strumpet. Both Adrian and Miss Baylor had assumed she was Charles Leight's mistress! She swore she had given them no reason to doubt her morals. So Miss Baylor had seen Mr. Leight briefly embrace her. Well, they were practically cousins by marriage. If the woman had no more confidence in her power over her betrothed, perhaps she shouldn't have been marrying him.

As for Adrian, what had he ever witnessed other than a few friendly exchanges between her and his cousin? The man was completely unreasonable. Likely he had been prejudiced against her by his mother from the start. She was an American. She sketched nude statues. Naturally, it must follow that she would take a lover at the drop of a hat.

"Your hair needs only a few extra pins." The maid went to a table and picked up several spare ones. "Don't worry. We'll have you back out on the dance floor in two shakes."

"Actually, I'm still not feeling quite the thing," Maeve said. The statement wasn't entirely untruthful. Her stomach was in knots. In the ballroom, she'd be filled with dread that Miss Baylor would expose her and Adrian and he would be obliged to marry her. The last thing she wanted was a forced marriage to a man who took her for a trollop—especially when she happened to be in love with him and he remained indifferent to her.

Her throat tightened, and she swallowed hard. "Is it at all possible for you to have a footman procure a respectable hackney cab for me?"

The young woman's freckled brow creased. "Ah, Miss, we can't have you going home alone. Let me fetch a relative or friend for you. Did you come here with your mother—or perhaps an aunt?"

"An aunt, but I don't want to spoil her evening. I assure you I shall be quite safe. I need only to travel to South Audley Street."

The maid wrung her hands, but after a moment she smiled. "I'll tell you what, Miss. South Audley Street is just around the corner. I reckon I can get the duchess's coachman to drive you there in two shakes. Traffic shouldn't even figure at this time of night. But let me summon your aunt so you can tell her your plans. Otherwise, she'll be sick with worry."

Maeve nodded. "You're right."

The woman procured two footmen, sending one to the stables and one to look for the countess.

Maeve sank down on a nearby chair and scoured her brain for a way to assure Aunt Eleanor that she needn't leave with her. Truly, she wanted nothing more than solitude at this point. It hurt too much to mix with the world. People assumed the worst of you—or failed to live up to your expectations of them.

Why had Adrian believed her Mr. Leight's lover, and

why had he thought to broach the subject with her? Inexplicably, he'd said he didn't mean to censure her. What had he been leading up to before Miss Baylor had interrupted?

Perhaps an offer to take her on as his own mistress.

She bit her lower lip. How foolish she'd been to suppose he would ever want to marry her. She should have learned more from her experience with Thomas. Well, she would never again count her chickens before they were hatched. She would never presume she had the love or respect of any man.

Emotionally exhausted, she slumped back in her chair. Thank goodness she would be home soon.

She would not leave the house again for a long time.

# Fourteen

Adrian circled the entire house but neither found Maeve nor heard news of her from several servants whom he saw and questioned. Evidently she'd gone back into the ballroom after all—or into another part of the house. Unfortunately, he couldn't confirm it, because but now he was too wet to present himself. He could only hope she hadn't done something truly daft, such as trying to walk home.

A large drop of water slipped from an eave above him and splattered on top of his head.

"Damnation!" He ran a hand over his damp hair. Though the rain remained a drizzle, the thought of Maeve walking the streets alone was more than enough to concern him.

*I'd best get the barouche and take a look beyond the grounds, just in case,* he thought.

Turning around, he ran to the stables he'd directed his coachman to use. A lad tending horses there offered to fetch his man from the Baylors' servants' hall.

Adrian declined. "I won't need him. I'll be returning directly."

The young servant helped him ready his horses, and in no time he was on the road. He took the fastest route to South Audley Street and saw scarcely any pedestrians along the way, only a vagabond and three raucous young drunks, singing as they staggered along the pavement.

Knowing that Maeve could have met with the likes of them—or worse—he felt a shiver run down his spine. If anything had happened to her, he'd never forgive himself for allowing her to slip away. Though Miss Baylor's bizarre caper had spurred her flight, he knew *he* had been the chief cause of her distress. Surely he could have found a more diplomatic way to broach the topic of her affair with Charles . . . although one hardly expected a woman serving as a mistress to be missish about it.

He picked up the pace, keeping his ears and eyes alert. The night seemed unusually quiet, which he hoped was a good sign. Within minutes he had traversed the few blocks to Lady Blaine's house. After tying the horses with a haphazard knot, he took the front steps two at a time and banged at the door.

The wait for someone to answer felt interminable. When the butler finally came, he looked concerned. "Your grace—here at this hour? How may I help you?"

"Webster, has Miss Irvine—that is, *have* Miss Irvine and the countess returned from the Baylors' ball?"

"No, your grace. I don't expect them home for hours yet." He frowned. "Can I deliver a message to them for you? If the matter is urgent, I can send a messenger around to the Baylors' residence."

"No, no, that won't be necessary. I'm on my way there now."

Webster raised an eyebrow but scarcely missed a beat before bowing. "As you please, your grace."

Hoping that he hadn't alarmed the man, Adrian dashed back to the barouche. He followed a different route to the Baylors' and still didn't encounter Maeve. Most likely she was safely on the dance floor or refreshing herself with her aunt—but of course he wouldn't be able to rest until he'd verified her whereabouts.

Upon reaching the stables again, he remembered that yesterday before the picnic he'd left a spare jacket inside the barouche. While the stable hand took care of his horses, he ducked inside the equipage and changed.

As he stashed his wet jacket under one of the benches, something hard grazed his hand—Maeve's sketchbook. He'd hidden it there earlier that evening, planning to return it to her after the ball. Now that he would be parting with it shortly, he had a strong urge to peek inside. He knew he shouldn't invade her privacy, but he still felt her art might give him the insight into her character that he desperately needed. She had always promised she would allow him to view the sketchbook soon. Hadn't he waited long enough?

There was no time for debating. He pulled out the volume and opened it to the first page.

He found himself aboard a ship on the ocean. Directly before him a section of iron rail sprouted up from a weather-beaten wooden deck. Beyond that, he saw nothing but wave after rolling wave. No land. No gulls flying overhead. Not even a jumping fish to break up the undulating sea. Far in the distance, a sole wisp of a cloud floated over the ocean.

Staring at the scene, he felt a tug of loneliness. At the bottom of the page, he discerned a single faint word penciled in one corner: *Emptiness*. The date confirmed that she had drawn the seascape during her transatlantic voyage.

He gulped and flipped the page. That, and several following, depicted other seafaring scenes, each labeled with a lightly scratched title at the bottom. In a spray of seawater crashing onto the deck of a ship, he found the word *Tumult.* One fanciful sketch—at least he presumed it was fanciful—showed a horrific tentacle flailing from the water. In the murky depths from which the limb emerged, a hint of a bestial eye lurked. The title read *The Unknown.*

The sketches told him not only what Maeve had seen on her voyage but what she had felt: loneliness, turmoil, fear of the unknown. Her coming to England had taken even more courage than he had guessed. Regretting that he didn't have time to dwell on each image, he continued skimming.

On one page, he scanned a page of notes she had jotted on the nature of art. He wished he had leisure—and the right—to study her philosophical views.

A little further into the book, she had written a short, untitled poem. At first he hesitated to peruse the verses without her permission, but in the end curiosity proved too hard to resist. He read the following:

*A specter of comfort visited me*
*In the winter of my sorrow*
*With promises of love*
*When I needed to be loved*
*When I had little hope for the morrow.*

*I fancied my regard reflected in his eyes*
*But it was only the allure of gold.*
*And when another came along*
*With expectations more strong*
*The fervor of his suit went cold.*

Adrian frowned and reread the words. He didn't understand all of the references, but he gathered enough to know that she had been deeply disappointed in love—*before he'd ever met her.* Perhaps a broken heart had precipitated the wanton tendencies she demonstrated now. He wondered if there were a chance she would heal and reform herself. Surely if he himself could come to think of love again, anyone had hope.

He turned his attention to the page facing the poem, where she'd drawn a man surrounded by chests of coins, jewelry, and gold bars. The caption read, *Thomas—with his true love.* Clearly this was the man who had who had robbed her of her innocence— likely in more ways than one.

As he stared into the pale eyes of the subject, heat rose under his collar. The fellow's wan complexion and colorless hair added no warmth to a face that might have been chiseled in ice. The flawless structure of his features had probably once appealed to the artist in Maeve.

No longer able to enjoy the artwork, he sped through the next dozen or so pages. The only sketches he paused to study were two surprisingly flattering portraits of himself and several charming drawings of Eliza.

Finally he came to the portrait of Charles. He gazed at the bovine expression on his cousin's face and could almost taste his own bitterness.

*Insipid coxcomb,* he thought, his jaw tensing. *Surely she cannot prefer that idiot to me.*

He flipped to the following page, only to be confronted with the male nude he had glimpsed during the picnic. This time, however, he got a better look. Immediately he noticed that the face didn't resemble Charles's.

Had Maeve taken yet another lover? For a split second his stomach tightened.

Then he saw the title at the bottom of the page: *Lysippus's Hercules.* Understanding dawned on him. She had taken the likeness from a statue, not a living model.

He practically clapped his hand on his forehead. Suddenly her indignation at his earlier accusations made sense. She had never drawn his cousin nude! In all likelihood, Charles was merely her admirer and not her lover.

*How on earth could I have made such a mistake?*

He peered more closely at the figure. The lack of clothing precluded quick identification, and Maeve had rendered the hair rather too realistic for a statue. Still, the archetypal contraposto stance and the classic straight-nosed profile shouted ancient Greek styling. His ignorance really couldn't be excused.

A combination of mortification and relief flooded through him. No wonder Maeve had been offended by his upbraiding her at the picnic, let alone by the accusations he'd unleashed tonight. What a prude she must have thought him for condemning her for nothing more than drawing a Greek statue. And what a cad for doubting her virtue!

Damn it, he had to speak to her—at once.

He clapped the book shut and shoved it back under the bench. He needed to get her alone, to talk to her without interruption until they'd hashed out the truth of their feelings for one another. Quite probably, he would have to tell her all about Belinda in hope that his candor would lead her to share her own hopes and fears. Once both of their histories had been laid bare, he hoped he would have a better idea if his suit held the least chance with her.

*I do want to marry her,* he finally acknowledged.

Within five minutes he had returned to the ballroom, not even caring that his dry blue jacket didn't match his formal black breeches.

A scene even more chaotic than before met him. The room was louder, hotter, and more crowded. Luck was with him, however. Almost directly, he spotted Lady Blaine and his mother, chatting with Lord Paterson and Colonel Westfall. The foursome sipped from champagne saucers and laughed uproariously at something the colonel said.

"Adrian, where have you been?" his mother asked as he joined them. She had none of her usual meddlesome air, however. On the contrary, she grinned at him broadly. "You've missed all of the excitement."

He ignored her comment. "Have you seen Miss Irvine recently?"

"I'm afraid that Maeve developed a headache." Lady Blaine turned to him. "Actually, when the maid summoned me to her, I was surprised you weren't keeping her company. Anyway, she went home a quarter hour ago."

A wave of fear rippled through him. "How did she go home? Are you sure she's safe?"

"She'll be fine. Our hosts very kindly offered her transport, but I sent her home with my own coachman and carriage. Lord Paterson has generously agreed to drive me home."

He nodded absently. Thank heavens Maeve hadn't tried to walk home or accepted a ride from a stranger.

Lady Blaine looked at his mother. " 'Tis doubly unfortunate that Maeve should have a headache tonight of all nights, isn't it, Jane? She really ought to have been present for Charles's announcement."

"The duke may not even be aware of what passed." Lord Paterson stepped closer to him. "Your grace, did you hear your cousin announce his betrothal?"

"Why, no." Adrian blinked in shock. Charles was to be married? And, obviously, not to Maeve? "Whom is he to marry?"

"Miss Baylor." His mother lifted her hands, palms up. "Can you credit it? I must say that he rose to the occasion nicely, too, Adrian. He presented the bride-to-be with a magnificent portrait of himself. Adding to the surprise, it turns out that our Miss Irvine is the artist."

*Maeve* had done Charles' portrait as a gift for his fiancée? He frowned. "Did Miss Irvine know that he intended to present the portrait to Miss Baylor?"

"Of course," Lady Blaine answered. "Your cousin confided in both of us but swore us to secrecy. Thank goodness the cat is out of the bag now. I never liked the idea of keeping something so important from all of our closest acquaintances."

"What about Miss Baylor—did she know that Charles had commissioned the portrait?" Adrian probed further. If the young woman had shared his ignorance, she might also have shared his misconceptions about Maeve's relationship to Charles. Unchecked jealousy might have accounted for the ridiculous prank she had pulled on them.

"She couldn't have been more surprised. The poor creature was hard-pressed to control her emotions. After a moment, she actually ran out of the room, and Mr. Leight had to go after her." His mother shook her head. "I still can't believe that I saw none of this coming. I had thought Charles was courting Miss Irvine. He'd been spending so much time with her. It turns out she was only taking his likeness."

*At least you didn't assume they were having an affair,* Adrian thought, disgusted with himself.

"Oh, and I forgot to mention that Miss Irvine painted the portrait as a betrothal gift," his mother added. "Charles intended to pay her, but she refused any compensation—quite a grand gesture, given her financial circumstances."

He grimaced, his sense of guilt multiplying by the second.

"Maeve really has no need to paint for money," Lady Blaine said, casting her gaze downward.

"Excuse me," he said. "I have to go."

"If you're looking for Charles, he's there." His mother pointed toward a mass of people swarming like bees on a hive. "I daresay you'll have trouble getting near him. Everyone is eager to congratulate him."

Disregarding her, he turned toward Colonel Westfall. "Sir, would you mind escorting my mother home tonight? I have some pressing business I need to attend."

Westfall glanced at the duchess and looked back to Adrian. "It would be my pleasure."

"Thank you. Good night to all of you." He turned and darted into the crowd.

"Just a minute, Adrian," his mother called after him. "Where are you going?"

Disregarding her, he took a shortcut through the terrace doors and ran back out to the stables. Again he enlisted the stable hand to help him ready the horses. He tipped the boy generously. Then for the second time within the hour, he rushed toward the house on South Audley Street.

When Maeve dragged her drooping body into her aunt's house, she was surprised to find the butler in the front hall at such a late hour.

He looked up from the floral arrangement he was tidying. Strangely, his face showed no sign of surprise at seeing her. "Good evening, Miss. The Duke of Ashton was here not long ago looking for you and Lady Blaine."

Her whole body tensed. What more could Adrian possibly have to say to her? Hadn't he hurt her enough?

She swallowed. "Did he leave a message?"

Webster shook his head. "He said he was returning to the Baylors' ball and would find you there."

Relief washed through her. "Good. He'll find my aunt, who is far better suited to speak to him."

He cocked his head in a doubtful manner. "I suppose so."

She walked past him toward the staircase. "If by some chance the duke should return, tell him I've retired for the evening. I have a headache and don't wish to be disturbed."

"I'm sorry, Miss. Is there anything I can get you? Perhaps a glass of wine would help you sleep."

She hesitated. "You may be right—but Auntie left a decanter in the drawing room earlier this evening. I'll pour myself a glass. Thank you for the suggestion."

He bowed. "My pleasure, Miss."

"Good night." She stepped into the drawing room.

The large, dark space afforded a comforting contrast to the crowded glare of the ball. She poured a large glass of claret and sat down in a plush chair before the fireplace. Earlier a roaring blaze had warmed the room, and the remaining coals still glowed in the grate. An occasional flame flared and died.

She leaned back in the chair and closed her eyes, trying to calm her nerves. So her hopes had once again been dashed. The experience was nothing new to her. She was no worse off than she'd been when she had first set foot on English soil only a few weeks ago.

The thought of that day brought back inopportune memories of meeting Adrian. How carefree they had both seemed during that initial encounter.

Why did carefree moments always have to be so fleeting and times of misery so difficult to shake off?

The sound of soft footsteps behind her broke the silence. Webster must have returned to check on her. She looked over her shoulder and found Adrian approaching. Her heart seemed to jump in her chest.

"Hello, Maeve," he said quietly.

She swung around in her chair to face him without getting up. "What are you doing here? I told Webster not to admit you."

"I was afraid you might do that, so I let myself in." He held up a key and sat down in a chair adjacent to her. "Lady Blaine and I exchanged these after Eliza was born. There are occasions when one of us needs to fetch something for the baby from the other's residence."

"Excellent." She turned back around and stared into the hearth. "Give me one good reason I shouldn't have Webster throw you out this minute. And don't tell me that my reputation is at stake if I'm discovered here with you. I don't care a fig about my reputation."

"Well, for one thing, I have your sketchbook with me."

Her gaze shot back to him, and she saw that he indeed had the leather volume. She held out her hand. "Pray return my property immediately."

He handed her the book.

She pulled her gaze away from his and opened the volume, flipping through the leaves. "Is everything here, or did you take it upon yourself to destroy the drawings you deemed unfit for a young female?"

"Of course not! I would never destroy any of your work. Your sketches are beautiful—all of them."

"You didn't seem to think so yesterday at the picnic." She snapped the book shut and looked back up at him. "Did you view all of them, then?"

"Yes." He took a deep breath. "I hope you don't mind. I cannot tell you what an impression they made. I would love to spend some time telling you just how each drawing affected—"

"Oh, no." She hugged the book against her bosom. "I've had quite enough of your art criticism. I drew these sketches for no one but myself, and I refuse to debate the subject matter with you or anyone else."

"I have no intention of criticizing your art or anything else about you." He leaned forward, resting his elbows on his knees. "I was out of line yesterday, and even more so this evening. I thought . . . well, let's just say I was being stupid."

She shook her head slowly. "I'm tired of your berating me, then trying to charm me into forgetting how surly you can be. You can't do it anymore." Getting out of her chair, she started out of the room. "Good night."

"Wait." He rose and strode up behind her, stopping her with a hand on her shoulder. "I have far more to apologize for."

The heat of his touch filled her with longing for more. Closing her eyes, she gave a shudder that threw off his hold. Without turning around, she said, "It makes no difference."

"I know how mistaken I was about you and my cousin. I can't even express my mortification. Charles presented your portrait of him to Miss Baylor just after you left the ball. I didn't have a chance to see the work myself, but by all accounts, everyone was awed."

Learning that the secret was out brought a rush of emotion that surprised her. Her throat closed up. Still refusing to face him, she shrugged.

"Maeve, there's no excuse for my assumptions about you, but before you entirely forswear my acquaintance, I need you to understand something about my past." His clothing rustled as he took a step away. "There's a reason I'm rather more distrustful that I ought to be. You see . . . Belinda wasn't faithful to me."

Her jaw fell open. She spun around and found him

looking into the fireplace. "Are you . . . are you certain?"

He stooped down and picked up the poker, prodding at the coals. "Quite. She told me herself, when I returned from the war. She confessed that she was with child and didn't know whether or not I was the father."

A million impressions raced through her mind: her aunt's hints that Belinda had been spoiled and self-absorbed, the poor woman's unwavering support of Adrian despite his desertion of her daughter. She blinked rapidly to try to hold back her tears. "You, mean that . . . Eliza . . ."

For a moment he was still. At last, he set down the poker and stood again, meeting her gaze. "Right."

She felt sick. "But surely she is yours. She has the look of you . . . and of your mother."

"I hope you're right. Not that it matters much anymore. She's mine in all the most important ways. The point is that my marriage left me a bitter, suspicious man. It still doesn't absolve me for what I thought about you and Charles, but I hope it will help you understand how I was thinking. I sensed that you were being secretive, and I assumed the worst. I can only beg you to forgive me."

"No, no, this is all my fault." She put her hands up to her face. Her cheeks felt hot with shame. "As you pointed out, you merely sensed my lack of candor. My painting Mr. Leight's portrait isn't the only thing I've been hiding. When I moved here, I decided to hide my wealth as well. The truth is that I have a considerable fortune. I have no need pursue a living painting."

It was his turn to gape. "Are you saying your livelihood isn't dependent on Lady Blaine?"

She shook her head and sank down on a footstool in front of the chair she had vacated. "You're not the only one who has been wounded by love—if indeed one can call it love. Last year, shortly after my father's death, I accepted an offer of marriage from a young man I'd known for years. Naturally, the wedding couldn't take place until my mourning period had ended. However, a month after entering the engagement, Thomas—that's his name—reneged on his offer. Within weeks he married a young heiress, one with a larger fortune than I."

Adrian said nothing for a long moment. When he spoke, it was through clenched teeth. "You chose not to sue him for breach of contract?"

"That would only have brought me further humiliation. The betrothal had never been announced, so I don't even know if I would have had a case."

Another moment lapsed, then he let out a snort. "If this revelation weren't so painful, it would be almost comical. Can you credit that at one time I actually suspected you were after Lady Blaine's money? Please don't take that bit of stupidity personally. Remember, I have a distrustful nature. If this experience doesn't teach me to be rational, nothing will."

A surprised laugh slipped out of her. "You know, you're right. It is rather comical. Given all of the time that you and I have spent together, we still haven't come to know each other very well, have we?"

"I beg to differ. We've come to know each other very well—now, anyway." He knelt down on the floor beside her. "Maeve, until I met you, I had never confided the story of Belinda's betrayal to anyone—not even Denny, and heaven knows he's always wondered why I went back to the war at such a time. I've often suspected that Lady Blaine and my mother may know, but I've never brought myself to broach the subject with them."

"Well, I'm glad that you felt you could confide in me tonight." She looked downward, unnerved by the intensity of his gaze—and their conversation. "I'm glad my secret is out, too."

"'Tis ironic that when you and I met, I had the mistaken impression that I knew you," he said softly. "When I realized the truth, my sense of knowing you never really faded. All along I've treated you with more familiarity than I was entitled to—taken liberties I shouldn't have."

She looked up at him, and the smile he gave her nearly made her melt. Just thinking about the times he had kissed her made her yearn to feel his mouth on hers again. Embarrassed, she cast her gaze into her lap. "Obviously, I didn't mind as much as I should have."

He took her hands in his, his fingers strong and warm. "Maeve, I was so jealous when I thought you preferred Charles to me. You do not prefer him, do you?"

She laughed, giddy to hear such a confession from him. Could he possible have serious feelings about her after all? Afraid to hope, she murmured, "Of course not."

"What about . . . Thomas, wasn't it? Do you still carry a torch for him?"

Looking him in the eye, she held his gaze. The emotion she read in his face sent a tingle down her spine. She took a deep breath. "I believe you know who it is I carry a torch for."

"I can hope." He took both her hands in one of his and raised the other to touch her cheek. "Dearest Maeve, pray renounce your vow never to marry and agree to become my wife."

Her throat constricted again. Unable to speak, she nodded vigorously.

"Oh, Maeve." He took her in his arms and squeezed her. "You've made me the happiest of men."

She reached around his broad shoulders and reveled in his strength, in the security she felt in his embrace. "Then I'll do all I can to keep you that way. I promise."

He pulled back and looked at her. "And I promise to do all I can to make you feel prized, like Helen of Troy. I never want to hear you compare yourself to Cressida again."

"You shan't. Lately, I've begun to tire of Cressida and her fickle ways." She smiled. "From now on, I believe I shall be completely content to be Maeve—so long as I always have you to play opposite me."

"In every scene," he assured her.

"I love you, Adrian," she said, unafraid and unembarrassed.

He grinned. "I love you, too."

"Then kiss me before one of the servants looks in and throws you out of the house."

"If any servant dares come in, I'll dispatch him or her for more wood for the fire." He pulled her into his arms again. "I'm not going anywhere."